THE
RETURN
OF
DEATH ERIC

THE
RETURN
OF
DEATH ERIC

SAM LLEWELLYN

Walker & Company

NEW YORK

Published in the United States of America in 2006 by Walker Publishing Company, Inc.
Distributed to the trade by Holtzbrinck Publishers

First published in the United Kingdom in 2005 by the Penguin Group, Puffin Books

For information about permission to reproduce selections from this book, write to
Permissions, Walker & Company, 104 Fifth Avenue, New York, New York 10011

Library of Congress Cataloging-in-Publication Data
Llewellyn, Sam.
The return of Death Eric / Sam Llewellyn.
p.   cm.
Summary: Convinced that a raven has cursed him with bad luck, Eric Thrashmettle ends his career as leader
of Death Eric, the best rock band in the universe, and becomes an embarrassment to his two children who,
when they realize that the family's finances are suffering, plot to get him back on the stage for a comeback.
ISBN-10: 0-8027-8951-X • ISBN-13: 978-0-8027-8951-8
[1. Rock music—Fiction. 2. Musicians—Fiction. 3. England—Fiction. 4. Humorous stories.] I. Title.
PZ7.L7723Ret 2006   [Fic]—dc22   2006044718

Visit Walker & Company's Web site at www.walkeryoungreaders.com

Printed in the United States of America by Quebecor World Fairfield

2 4 6 8 10 9 7 5 3 1

All papers used by Walker & Company are natural, recyclable products
made from wood grown in well-managed forests. The manufacturing processes
conform to the environmental regulations of the country of origin.

For
Nick
Fran and Kieran
Bunk Dogger
Paranoia Jones
Dicky Hart
and
The Organ

INTRO

The main stage at the Chickenstock Festival is the biggest stage at the biggest music festival in the world. The raven that was flying over it that night just after sunset was old, wise for a raven, and not impressed.

To the raven, the main stage looked like the glint in a gigantic eyeball. It stopped flapping its wings, spread the finger-feathers on the end, and began a long, sweeping glide. From below, there came the tramp of a heartbeat, slowing, and the moan of an animal in pain, maybe a giant buffalo. Slowing heartbeats are of great interest to ravens. They are all part of the food situation.

On the stage, Eric Thrashmettle exchanged glances with Fingers Trubshaw (bass guitar) and Kenyatta McClatter (drums). Death Eric, the world's foremost feedback metal band, were slowing it right, right down. Eric's guitar was moaning away over the top. This was the end of Part One of their triple-platinum song "Pig Train." This was where it died away and nearly stopped, ready to come crashing back in again for Part Two, brisk and cheery as an air strike on a tank regiment.

Ravens are not musical. As far as the raven was concerned, what was going on down there was that something very big was dying, which meant a very large supper, and probably lunch tomorrow as well.

Eric Thrashmettle made large waving movements with his guitar neck, tripped over his feet, and stamped on his big red pedal. The guitar sobbed and howled. The sound tumbled into the night. Half a million people held their breath. They all knew the song. They were waiting for Part Two. A gust of wind bowled out of the dark hills and stirred the scarves tied to the mike stands. The guitar note died away.

With a dry rustle of feathers, the raven swooped out of the darkness and perched, blinking, on the microphone.

Now that it was here, it was rather disappointed. There was nothing within range that looked all that edible. It tried with a brain the size of a garden pea to make things add up. It had no luck.

The final howl of "Pig Train" Part One died away. Eric gazed at the raven with a fixed expression on his dead-white face. His mouth hung open. The silence lengthened.

Death Eric was the biggest, loudest, headbangingest, most outrageous rock-and-roll band in the known universe. It had practically invented bad behavior. The rumors about the musicians' private lives were so dreadful that it was illegal for anyone under eighteen to repeat them. Some rock-and-roll bands eat live bats onstage. Death Eric ate anything that breathed, and quite a lot of things that did not.

Birds did not stand on microphones and . . . *just look* . . . at bands this big.

"Oi!" hissed Fingers Trubshaw (bass), sidling toward his leader. Eric had been a rocker since anyone could remember, so Eric tended to forget where he was from time to time.

Normally, Eric would have jumped three feet straight up in the air and gone into Part Two. But tonight, he stood and stared at the raven, his legendary guitar, Rabid Dingo, silent in his hand.

The raven stared back. It was wise, for a raven. But ravens are only birds, so actually it was pretty stupid.

Fingers Trubshaw raised his arm. If hissing at Eric did not work, a huge fuzz bass chord might.

In the crowd, hundreds of thousands of hands fumbled in hundreds of thousands of anorak pockets. Hundreds of thousands of arms rose above hundreds of thousands of heads. *Scritch*, went hundreds of thousands of gritty little lighters.

In the raven's eye there appeared hundreds of thousands of tiny flames. A great chant began. *Pig Train*, it went. *Püg Train.*

Not surprisingly, the raven freaked right out.

"Awk," it said. Then it spread its wings and flapped into the air.

It seemed to hover for a moment above Eric

Thrashmettle, its feathers dusty black in the lights. Eric watched it, hypnotized.

It is never a good idea to watch a frightened bird from underneath. Frightened birds can lose control. This one certainly did. Right in Eric's left eye.

"Rrrrrgh," said Eric Thrashmettle, pawing with a skinny hand at a face the color of chalk and raven dung.

Kenyatta McClatter gave his drums a batter. Fingers Trubshaw hit the Planetsmasher switch. The intro to Part Two roared on to the bit where Eric came in.

Eric just stood there, shaking his head.

Then he turned to run away.

But the exit was blocked by Enid the Roadie.

He turned the other way.

But the exit was blocked by Sid the Soothsayer.

Tearing Rabid Dingo from around his neck, Eric Thrashmettle made a run for it. Mistaking a huge black speaker cabinet for a door, he plunged in. The cloth front ripped. Electric roarings and buzzings came from the interior. An assistant roadie went after him. The crowd noise was like thunder. The laser show shot lightning bolts into the night. Fingers and Kenyatta brought the song to a close, watching the speaker cabinet out of the corners of their eyes. The lights went out. In the blackness, three strong roadies carried Eric back to his trailer and mopped his eye and gave him a nice glass of milk and went away, locking the door on the outside.

Eric sat and stared at the door. "Woooh," he said from time to time.

Five minutes later, it opened. A gray-haired man in a gray silk suit, a gray silk shirt, and silver lizardskin cowboy boots of impeccable cut came in. "Nice set," he said in a smooth gray voice.

Eric looked up, wild-eyed behind his round red glasses. "There was a bird," he said.

"Birds will be birds," said the man in gray soothingly.

His name was Per Spire, alias the Management. His job was to soothe Death Eric, and to deal with the business, and to organize the tours and the recording sessions, and to arrange for the roadies to drive the big lorries with the gear, and to stop Eric from putting his eye out with the cutlery at mealtimes.

"It like looked at me," said Eric.

"Surely not," said Per smoothly.

"It, like, flapped out of the dark and, like, looked at me and then it, like, flapped off again."

"Gone now," said Per, smiling his smooth smile.

"The bird is gone," said Eric, rubbing his left eye. "The curse, like, remains."

"Ho, ho," said Per, waving a hand with badly bitten nails.

"Lo," said Eric. "I shall play no more."

"'No more'?" said Per. "New song? Nice title."

"I shall not play, like, never. For I am cursed."

"Dear, dear me," said Per, secretly examining his hands for a fingernail of biteable length and finding he had used them all up.

"My career," said Eric Thrashmettle, "has been ended by a message from, like, Beyond. I hereby retire."

"Dearie, dearie me," said Per again.

Perhaps one of the roadies had some nails. But biting other people's nails was not really much good. You needed your own.

The raven stood on a standing stone and watched the lights of the artics and limousines wind away into the hills.

It was not thinking about curses. Actually, it did

not even know what curses were. It was thinking about food, as usual. It was disappointed not to have found the giant buffalo.

Still, with all this traffic, there would be plenty of dead rabbits on the highway.

Welcome aboard the bus, ladies and gentlemen, boys and girls. And here we go, passing through the huge iron gates of the Costa de Lott estate, home of the startlingly rich. Note the trim green lawns. Note the golfers in their gold-plated Rolls-Royces. Note the large bushes covered in tropical flowers, and the huge houses, white stucco and red brick, crouched eaves-deep in the foliage.

The *what*?

The *leaves*, my dear. This is a tour for people who speak English. Now if you would be so good as to direct your eyes out of the window, little missy. On your left, Froufrou Lodge, home of Spiridion Flounce, the millionaire dress designer. On your right, sonny, Das Bunker, new home of Ermenegildo Ponque, the Odd Dictator. And coming up right ahead . . . well, you will note that plenty of the windows are broken and there is a yin-yang flower bed and no, madam, that is not a fridge but a 1,000-watt guitar amplifier half buried in the lawn as if flung from an upper window by someone very strong. Yes, indeed, little girl, or as you say, very mad. For this is Dunravin, the house of—

KERRRRANNNNNGGGGGGG, roared a huge metal voice somewhere in the sky. Glass burst from a window and pattered onto the patio.

—as I was saying, the house of—

KAJJJOOOOOOOONNGGGGGGGG, bellowed the metal voice.

—the world's numero uno rock 'n' roll hero, idolized by billions, whose song "Pig Train" has been adopted as the anthem of Olympic Games and more shopping mall openings than you have had—

WOOOOOOOOOOOOAARRRRNNNG

—school lunches. I refer, ladies and gentlemen, boys and girls, to the one and only Eric Thrashmettle. And by the Lord Harry, there he is!

At an upper window is a pale oval face, hardly visible between curtains of black hair. It is wearing bloodred spectacles. Who knows what lies behind that face, what deep thoughts it hides?

The answer to this question is not really any thoughts—

KARRRRROOOOOOOOOOOOOOOOOOOOOOOO

—because Eric never was much of a thinker, even in the far-off time when he had been plain Eric Smith, the most absentminded plumber's mate in Manchester. Nowadays he has so many people working for him that he never lifts a finger except to play his guitar, and he does not do that much anymore, since he reckons he had a curse put on him by a black bird at a festival somewhere.

The face has vanished from the window. It will now be stumbling around the room, bumping into things. And there in the drive in front of the front door are a boy and a girl somewhere between the ages of ten and thirteen, climbing into a long black Cadillac. The girl is wearing an elegantly tailored suit, with sensible but attractive shoes. Her bedroom, which she has just left, is hung with priceless antique tapestries. In the middle of the floor is the great vivarium containing her reptile collection. On the only wall not hung with tapestries is a bookcase, filled with leather-bound novels and books of stories. She loves to read. At school, she comes somewhere around the top of the class in English, Music, and Reptile Appreciation. She is prettyish and has glossy dark hair. Her eyes are green and have a look of deep understanding that makes people nervous. Her name is Lulubelle Flower Fairy Thrashmettle, but do not try calling her that, because she thinks it is silly, and she is right, as usual. Call her Lou.

Next to her is her brother. He is wearing black slacks of impeccable cut, a neat black blazer in the Italian style, and Gucci loafers. His bedroom, which he has just left, is walled with huge sheets of black slate, some of it covered in mathematical formulas. In the middle of the floor is a bear cage, vacant at the moment. Against the only unchalked wall is a long desk, covered with scientific instruments and small, glittering engines he has built. He loves to calculate. At school, he comes somewhere near the top of the class in Math, Science, and Bear Studies. He looks thin, shock-headed, and slightly haunted. His eyes are dark brown below the heavy brows and sometimes have an absent look, as if shiny little wheels are turning in far-off departments of his mind. His name is Living Buddha Thrashmettle, but do not try calling him that, because he already knows he is living, and he already knows he is not Buddha, who is a god, and he wants nothing to do with gods, and if this kid wants nothing to do with something, you had better believe that this is his final decision. Call him Buddy.

Buddy and Lou enter the car.

"Ready?" says Enid, at the wheel.

"Check," say Lou and Buddy crisply.

Enid Bracegirdle is the Main Roadie, and she has her head screwed on. Being a Main Roadie is like being the mother of a very large, unruly, and forgetful family. Enid is absolutely huge and very, very beautiful. She is wearing a print dress, for coolness, and big black boots, for usefulness. She gave up smoking three years ago, but she still does not find life easy. She puts a nicotine patch on her leg and her size-twelve workboot on the gas pedal. The Caddy drifts out of the driveway. They are going shopping. Ladies and gentlemen, boys and girls, this will be the first momentous step of a long, strange trip. So we will tag along.

"What d'you think of Dad?" said Lou.

"Not good," said Buddy. "Something's upset him."

"Blocked," said Lou.

"What?"

"He's got rocker's block. It's when you know how to play something but you just can't do it. Creative people get it all the time." She watched her brother closely. His dark eyes were brooding. She knew that look. She guessed that the word "creative" meant nothing to him. "Like when Mrs. Simms asked you to write a story called 'What I Did on My Holidays.'"

"Yeah, well, that," said Buddy, to whom stories were an annoying distraction from the serious business of equations. "That was because we went to some beach and they didn't tell us where we were, and when we got back we asked Dad where we'd been and he couldn't remember, and all the roadies were down the pub so I couldn't do the story."

"But I remember what you did. You asked the Management."

"Look, an Aston Martin."

"We have two in the garage," said Lou, who was much more interested in situations than machines. "Do not try to change the subject. What you do when you don't know something is talk to Management. That's how you wrote your story in the end. Management told you the beach name, and you were fine. So that's the kind of thing that's wrong with Dad. Obviously."

"Is that so?" said Buddy. Things that were obvious to his sister were not obvious to him. It worked the other way around, too.

Enid took the turn for City Center.

Nobody expected things to go right in the Thrashmettle household. But things seemed to be going even wronger than usual lately, thought Enid, giving a little old lady a V sign with one hand, painting its nails with the other, and steering around a corner with her big, tattooed knees. It was not Eric who was the problem, not any more than usual anyway. It was not Wave, the kids' mother, who was off doing yoga in Sweden, or was it the Philippines this time? It was not any one of the hairdressers, or the chief tattooist or his assistant or the assistant's assistant, or the pet cook or the snake vet or any of the cooks, drivers, guitar tuners, intensive-care nurses, and tree surgeons who catered to the minimum requirements of the Thrashmettle household. Enid hiked up her skirt a couple of inches so she could stick a new

…e patch above her right knee. No, she …t, what we have here is a failure of leadership at the center.

You could not in a billion years call Eric a leader, except of Death Eric, the grimmest and most deadly feedback metal band that had ever caused the world's ears to seep blood.

Leadership came from Management. Enid's tough but motherly mind softened, and her vision became pink and misty. In the mists, there floated a man in a gray silk suit with a gray silk shirt and silver lizardskin cowboy boots of impeccable cut. A man reclining in a gray leather armchair talking softly into a gray mobile phone, his gray hair arranged into a few careful spikes, nothing wild. A man with a gray face and eyes the grayish blue of tungsten steel, only harder. A man by the name of Per Spire, Swedish, mild as milk, solving all problems that were brought to him, and deadly as a five-mile cobra. In short, a manager; and (thought Enid) so, so lovable.

Eight years ago, Eric had formed the impression that he had been cursed by a raven at the Chickenstock Festival. It was now six months since anyone had seen Per Spire, but then (thought Enid) he was a man of subtle mind, noble and free, who often did things without telling anyone.

She looked out of the window. A man had come alongside in a convertible sports car. He was wearing a fur hat and smoking a cigarette. *Tch*, thought Enid, horrible habit. She leaned out of the limo window, picked the butt out of the man's mouth, and dropped it on his fur hat. The hat caught fire. Enid pulled a fire extinguisher from its bracket and hosed him down. Howls of rage came from inside the shapeless mass of foam and fumes. Enid rolled smoothly off as the light changed. Ahead loomed the spires and turrets of **SELFRODS**, the well-known department store.

"Shopping ahoy," said Lou, her green eyes glittering with pleasure.

Normally, Buddy would have brightened too. Visiting **SELFRODS**'s Books and Scientific Instruments Department was a reminder that in only two months, he and his sister would be leaving the shambles of Dunravin and going back to wonderful school. But today, Buddy's razor-sharp mind was preoccupied. Buddy liked things to add up, like sums and equations did. Today there was a problem without a solution.

The problem was this.

Not many people except his dad had candy-apple red Aston Martins. Even fewer people had candy-apple red Aston Martins bearing the number plate ER1K. Buddy particularly remembered the license plate, because Per had got it for his dad off the Queen of England. And that had been the license plate on the car he had seen out of the window while Lou had been babbling on about Management.

The Caddy drifted to a halt in front of **SELFRODS**. Men in top hats hastened to open the doors. Enid took out her knitting, climbed into the back of the car, turned on the TV, and tuned to a cooking program. Soon the kids would be back with their scientific instruments and uniforms, all excited about hard sums and blazers as usual, bless them.

But this morning, things were not as usual. Not at all.

It started off fine. In the Books and Scientific Instruments Department (where the children were well known) they filled a large shopping trolley with mighty volumes and complex devices. In the Uniforms Department, the assistant (who had watched them grow since their earliest years) helped them choose sublimely comfortable blazers in cashmere for autumn warmth—Venetian red for Lou, midnight black for Buddy. Then they set off for SELFRODS's famous Zoo.

It was in the Zoo that trouble struck.

SELFRODS's Zoo will sell its customers anything from a pygmy shrew to an African elephant, provided they have the moolah. Moolah had never been a problem for the Thrashmettle children. They pushed their deep-laden trolley over to the cages. Lou watched the pythons slithering over their sawdust floor. There was an Indonesian Squeezer in there that she really fancied. It had a beady but friendly eye, and she knew that your Indonesian Squeezer could grow to twelve yards long. She was very, very tempted.

Buddy, meanwhile, was by the Sumatran Snow Bear. He had always considered a bear a supremely logical animal—friendly, loyal, and big enough to eat a rock-and-roll star before a rock-and-roll star ate it, which was important, because when Buddy had been younger, he had had a lot of bad experiences with disappearing gerbils.

"Well?" said Lou.

"This one."

Lou came over, wrinkled her nose. "Bit niffy."

The bear did a winsome little dance, as if agreeing.

"Come and look at mine," said Lou. They went and stood in front of the pythons. "The kind-looking one," said Lou.

"Dad'll pinch it for his act. Remember the gerbils?"

"And the boomslang," said Lou.

It was a dark memory. She had been quite young when she had lost that charming boomslang, which had nonfatally bitten their father before vanishing into the plumbing of New York City's Chelsea Hotel.

"Ahem," said a voice. A man in a suit stepped out of the shopping throng. "Excuse me," he said. "I could not help overhearing all that about the gerbil and the boomslang and that. Have I the honor of addressing Flower Fairy and Living Buddha Thrashmettle?"

As members of a celebrity household, the Thrashmettle children were used to this sort of thing. Buddy's thumb went to the pager in his pocket. Both of them scowled heavily. "Who wants to know?" they said, in low, dark voices.

"Huggins," said the suit. "SELFRODS Security. Speaking personally, I am a great admirer of Death Eric, been to the concerts, got the T-shirts . . . I'll show you sometime if you're interested. Perhaps he could sign one?"

"He's busy that day," said Lou. "I should warn you that we are highly trained in Stranger Danger. Buddy?"

" 'Zackly," said Buddy, pressing the pager button and directing upon the security man a hostile glare. "Now if someone would please gift-wrap these wild beasts, we can proceed to the checkout."

"Er—," said the security man.

There was a thunder of workboots on SELFRODS parquet. Enid, summoned by the pager, hurtled into the room like a floral-print whirlwind, brandishing her knitting. She pushed the security man over and sat on him. An assistant arrived.

"As I was saying," said Lou. "We will take the Sumatran Snow Bear and the Indonesian Squeezer."

The assistant went an unusual shade of beet and started to sweat.

Enid's voice said, "Kids?"

The children turned toward her. The security

man's head was sticking out from under her skirts. His eyes were bulging and he was saying something in an undertone.

"There's a bit of a problem," said Enid, standing up and hauling the security man to his feet. "Mr. Huggins here tells me that, um, we can't pay."

Four eyes looked at her, two green, two dark brown. "I *beg* your pardon?"

Mr. Huggins stood up, wheezing. "The credit card company has asked me to take away your cards and cut them up."

"All right. We'll pay for this lot—"

"Not with your credit cards, you won't."

Lou tickled the Squeezer under its chin. She said, "But I've *bonded* with this python."

Buddy fondled an oscilloscope. He said, "But I *need* these instruments."

Mr. Huggins allowed himself to be dusted by Enid. "Then I suggest you complain not to me, but to whomever it is that pays the bills at your house."

"He's right, you know." Enid put her mighty arms around Buddy and Lou. "Come on, kids."

"So who does?" said Lou.

"Pay the bills, she means," said Buddy.

"Dunno," said Enid. "Come along. Lunchtime."

Leaving the piled trolley among the animal cages, they went.

In the car, Enid got on the phone, spoke for a while, then folded it up. "Hmm," she said.

"What?" said Lou, with a slight sinking feeling.

"There's no money left," said Enid.

"None?" said Buddy, appalled.

"None."

It was a slow, quiet drive home, everyone in the Cadillac wrapped in deep personal thoughts. And it was a thoughtful household that gathered for lunch around the enormous kitchen table.

"What we got, Cookie?" said Sid the Soothsayer, Death Eric's group fortune-teller.

"Guess," said Cookie.

"Bleep!" cried Flatpick the budgie from his cage.

Sid pulled a pocket-sized crystal ball from his belt pouch and peered into it deeply. "Steak 'n' kidney pie," he said in mystic tones. "Beans, chips, peas. Green salad, range of cheeses. Deep-dish apple pie with custard, option of bread-and-butter pudding. I might be wrong about the bread-and-butter pudding."

"Yeah, well," said Cookie. "Wrong as usual, *except* about the bread-and-butter pudding, which is partly right because we got bread, no butter, no pudding." He plunked a medium-sized loaf on the table. "Who wants to carve?"

"Sorry," said Sid to Enid.

"Nice try," said Enid insincerely. "Where's Eric?"

"He won't be coming down," said Sid the Soothsayer.

The kitchen door burst open and a disheveled figure appeared. "Breakfast!" said Eric. "I'm starving."

"It's lunch," said Lou. Last time she had seen her father, his hair had been black. Now it was green. This sort of thing was not unusual. She said, "You'll be starving when you've finished."

"Yeah," said Eric. "Nice. What's this?"

"Slice o' bread," said Enid.

"Nice," said Eric, digging in. He munched the bread with great enjoyment. "Cool," he said. "Well, er." He started to get up.

"Dad," said Lou. "Could you hang on a minute?"

"Who?" said Eric, looking around him in confusion. "Me?"

"You *are* our dad," said Buddy.

"Oh, hey, yeah, me, Dad. What do you need, fatherly advice? Money?"

"Both," said his children.

"Ooer," said Eric, nervously scratching the bat tattooed on his right triceps. "So?"

"What have you noticed about lunch?" said Lou.

"Everyone here," said Eric. "Nice."

"The food, though."

"Bread," said Eric. "Made with oats or barley or something. Beautiful. Seed in the ground, grows, makes more seed. Cut it down, shake it out, grind it up, put in some water and, er, dates or something—"

"Often," said Lou, with a sort of frozen patience, "we get more than bread for lunch, Dad."

"Have it, then," said Eric, beaming in a kindly manner. "This is Liberty Hall. Have whatever you want."

"How do we get it?" said Lou.

"Go to the shop, I dunno, int that what you do?"

"There's no money."

"Then get some."

"There isn't any. Anywhere."

Eric laughed heartily. "'Course there is. I saw someone spending some, when, last week, down the pub?"

Lou drew a deep, patient breath. "That was someone else. Who doesn't live here. Spending their money, not ours. Dad, the credit cards don't work, we can't buy instruments or uniforms or animals, and the cupboard is bare. We are skint."

"Oh dear," said Eric, yawning a bit. "Better ask Per, then."

"Per's not around."

"He'll be back," said Eric. He rose from his seat and walked into the wall. "Oof. Sorry, man," he said.

"Bleep!" cried Flatpick the budgie.

"The door is four and a half feet to your right," said Buddy. "By the way, what happened to your hair?"

"Hair?"

"It used to be black. Now it's green."

"Oh. I dyed it. Green."

"Ah."

"Nice one," said Eric, and left again, successfully this time.

"Hmm," said Enid. "Looks like it's up to us to make a plan."

Sid said, "I'm sure it'll all work out—"

"Shaddap," said the whole table at once.

It was at moments like this that Enid came into her own. She said, "There's a bit of gold buried in the garden. It'll tide us over. BB?"

"Here," said a small but muscular roadie.

She handed him a map that she drew from her mighty bosom. "X marks the spot," she said. "Get digging."

"Aye, aye," said BB.

There was a fierce pounding on the front door.

"What next?" said Enid, sighing. "Get it, will you, Needle?"

Needle was the Senior Tattooist. Teeth appeared in the blue tropical forest represented on his round, jolly face. He rolled out of the room. There was shouting, and a crash, and the crunch of large boots on English oak floorboards. Needle came back into the room, dribbled like a rugby ball by five enormous men with shaved heads and T-shirts with their sleeves rolled up to the armpit.

"ORRIGHT!" roared the biggest of the enormous men. "WE ARE THE BAILIFFS. YOU ARE IN SERIOUS TROUBLE. WE HAVE COME TO SEIZE GOODS TO THE VALUE OF"—he squinted at a piece of paper—"TWO HUNDRED AND FORTY THOUSAND. . . Cor, stone me, where did you get that tattoo?"

He was looking at Enid; in particular, Enid's right knee, on which was tattooed a merry ring-o'-roses of skeletons dancing around an electric guitar.

"Needle did it," said Enid, squeezing Buddy's hand under cover of the kitchen table.

"Course it did."

"That's Needle," said Enid, releasing Buddy's hand and pointing past his right ear. "He's a talented boy."

"She's right, you know," said Needle through a clatter of loose teeth.

"I want one too," said the big man.

Needle picked himself up, examined the bailiff critically, pursed his lips, and shook his head. "You're not gettin' it, are you?" he said. "Each of my works of art is original, distilled from the mood of the moment and the nature of the background skin. The reason I done skelingtons on Enid's knees is because Enid's knees *lend* themselves to skelingtons."

"Oh," said the big man, looking sulky.

"Whereas you," said Needle, "are more the naval anchor, heart o' love, dagger o' hate type person. Simple, traditional stuff. Am I right or am I right?"

The bailiff gazed upon him, shaking his head. "You are right," he said. "Plus, could you manage an elaborate scroll-type thing with MOTHER on it?"

"Just what I was goin' to suggest myself," said Needle. "Siddown, boys, while I round up my inks.

You other chaps, Cookie'll get you some, er, bread."

"We brought sandwiches," said the bailiffs. "Anyone fancy one? They're cheese."

They all sat around the table and had lunch. Afterward Enid shepherded the children away.

"Leave it to me," she said. "Meet again at teatime?"

"OK," said Buddy. As rock-and-roll kids, the Thrashmettles were used to slight emergencies. "We will be in the Blue Music Room."

There were several music rooms at Dunravin. There was the Black Room, dedicated to feedback and guitars distorted beyond recognition. There was the Keyboard Room, dedicated to . . . well, you get the idea. At the bottom of the garden, in a pavilion overlooking a round green pond full of educated goldfish, was the Blue Room. The Blue Room looked like a wedding cake turned inside out. White plaster animals strolled demurely across the blue background, and a couple of Greek goddesses draped in bandages gazed from the domed ceiling onto a grand piano and a cello.

"What a *relief*," said Lou, as the door thunked shut behind them. "What a *mess*."

Buddy scratched at his spiky black hair with a long, ink-stained finger. "No money?" he said.

"But Dad's got tons of it."

"Masses," said Lou.

"Though I suppose living like this is quite expensive."

"Private jets," said Lou.

"Everyone has them," said Buddy. While a genius at theory, he was not too good at the practical things in life.

"Enid'll have some ideas," said Lou.

"Probably," said Buddy, frowning. Enid was huge, kind, and as loyal as a mother wolf crossed with a bulldozer. If you wanted things done, Enid was the person to do them. But he was not sure about her as one of life's great planners. If you wanted plans made, you went to Per.

But nobody had seen Per for ages.

He looked narrowly at his sister as she rolled up her cream silk sleeves and plunked her cello with her slightly bitten fingers.

Mind you, Lou was quite a planner. And so was he.

"Music," he said, sitting down at the piano, "is the answer to all messes. A-one, two, *three*." And off they soared into the gauzy realms of *Bink's Music for Medium Length Afternoon*.

Some things are passed down from parents to

children and some are not. The Thrashmettle kids had avoided Eric's hotel-room-wrecking genes, his gerbil-eating genes, and his inability-to-remember-your-own-name-without-reading-the-special-tattoo-on-the-palm-of-your-hand genes. Happily for Lou and Buddy, the only gene that had hit home was the music gene. Lou could play any instrument with strings. Buddy could play any instrument with keys. Having been brought up since infancy in a roar of feedback metal, nowadays they naturally preferred classical, with occasional outings into Cool School jazz. (Not that they actively *disliked* feedback metal. It was just a little simpleminded and embarrassing. More than a little embarrassing, actually. But tremendously easy to play.)

So on they played, doing beautiful improvisations and twiddly bits, and the horrors of **SELFRODS** and the bailiffs dissolved into a sea of absolutely right notes played in absolutely the right order. Finally the piece ended.

"Very soothing," said Buddy. "Pure logic, in music form."

"And very beautiful," said Lou. She took a book from the special pocket of her coat and began to read.

"Not that again," said Buddy.

"This book is a constant source of useful notions," said Lou. "As you know."

"Indeed." Buddy steepled his fingers and gazed into space as his sister flicked through the pages of the volume. On the minus side, the *Tales from the Brothers Grime* were childish and silly. On the plus side, he had to admit that they had many times in the past offered solutions to severe problems. Though none as severe as this.

So Buddy waited in a state of mingled scorn and suspense.

"Got it," said Lou at last.

"You have?" said Buddy.

"'The Tale of the Ant and the House,'" said Lou. "An ant wanted to move a house away from the people inside it. And devised a means of so doing."

"Being?" said Buddy, frowning, as so often when Lou read from the *Tales*.

"Wait and see," said Lou infuriatingly.

The children walked back across the lawn to tea.

The kitchen contained an attractive smell of new cakes, Needle mopping bailiffs' blood off the table, Enid in front of a notebook with a telephone, a couple of roadies, some makeup artists, and a guitar tuner.

"We got rid of the bailiffs," said Needle. "Won't be back for a month, they said."

"And BB dug up the gold," said Enid. "Not as much of it as I hoped, but we can keep going for a month or two on basics. I've had to let the tree surgeons go, plus the snake vet, all but one of the guitar tuners, the intensive-care nurses, and all the roadies and humpers but six. Sad to see them go. Uniforms and scientific instruments are still out, I fear."

"And Per?"

"I've been phoning around. No sign of him. Not in his usual haunts. He's vanished." She shook her mighty head, hair swinging (she had it in dreadlocks this week). Enid did not do disappointed, but it would have been nice if Per had told her where he was going. "He could be anywhere in the world," she said with a sigh.

"Or off it," said Needle, swabbing.

"Wha?"

"He did that space tourism once," said Needle.

" 'Course he did," said Enid absently. "So it's typical, really. Don't worry, I'll be looking for him."

There was silence. Finally, Buddy said, "What a mess. I really, really hate messes."

Lou said, "What?"

"Messes. Illogical things. I hate them."

Lou's eyes were glittering like a pirate's emeralds. "What was that you were saying earlier?"

"Wha?"

"'Music is the answer to all messes,' you said."

Buddy's face cleared, as it always did when he saw a logical thread and followed it in one great leap. His dark eyes took on an electronic glow. "I see what you *mean*," he said.

Eric wandered into the kitchen, picked up the sponge cake, took a bite, wandered over to the window and fell out.

"Bleep!" cried Flatpick the budgie.

Lou found she did not want to say what she was going to say. She seemed to hear the squeak of threatened gerbils, the hiss of kidnapped snakes. She put these sounds firmly behind her. "We need money," she said. "So the band gets together again."

"The band?"

"Death Eric."

"Death *Eric*?" said everyone around the table except Enid, who was outside, disentangling Eric from the shrubbery. "The band's retired. Under a curse. It'll never get back together."

Lou raked with her green gaze the faces around the table, some human, some less so. "You mark my words," she said. "It will soon be back to work for all."

"Work?" they said. Shock and horror were printed on all faces except Needle's, which already had a jungle printed on it.

"We'll get 'em out on the road," said Buddy. "Tour. New album. The squids will come rolling in."

"Ladies and gentlemen," said Lou, standing on the table with one foot in a cake. "I present to you The Return of Death Eric!"

"Great," said everyone.

They definitely did not mean it.

Thanks to the gold in the garden, next morning the supply cupboards were full again. Breakfast was the usual hearty repast. Eric sat at the head of the table, eating a bowl of Coco Pops Coco Pop by Coco Pop. The staff did not join the Thrashmettles for breakfast, except Enid, who was more family than staff. Of course there was always a place laid for Wave, the children's mother, with her favorite organic sheep's yogurt and biodynamic honey. About once a year she turned up and ate it. Meanwhile, Enid was more of a mother to the children than Wave had ever been.

Enid finished her porridge, black pudding, eggs, chips, beans, sausage, tomato, kidneys, hash browns, bacon, and white and brown toast, all of it slathered in HP Sauce and washed down with several quart mugs of mahogany tea, four sugars. The children finished their cereal and tropical fruit. Enid reached over and scoffed Wave's yogurt.

"Right," said Eric. "I'm, er."

"Hold on," said Enid, putting a kind but mighty hand on his arm. "The nippers have got something to say to you."

"Nippers?" said Eric, frowning.

"Lou and Buddy," said Enid. "The green-eyed girl and the dark-haired boy."

"Us," said Lou and Buddy.

Eric's face broke into a beaming smile. "Hi!" he said, giving them a ring-crusted high five. "Wazzappening, smalls?"

"A lot," said Lou. "We told you yesterday. There's no money left."

"Ask Per," said Eric, frowning with concentration.

"We told you," said Buddy. "Per's not here."

"Oh." More frowning. Less concentration.

"And we've got an idea."

"Nice one!" More beaming.

"What we think," said Lou, nailing him with the bright green eyes, "*all* of us, and Mum would say the same thing if she was here, is, you've got to get the band back together."

Eric's jaw swung. "Uh?"

"Find Fingers and Kenyatta and go out on the road and be Death Eric and delight your millions of fans and play 'Pig Train' and get paid a fortune."

The curtains of Eric's hair fell together over his face so only his nose stuck out, like a white rock jutting from a green waterfall. "No," he said.

"If you don't, we'll starve."

"I'll get work," said Eric.

"Work?" said Enid. "What can you do?"

"Eat cheese," said Eric.

"Not a great way of making money."

"Make cheese."

"Better."

"But I dunno how."

"Ah. And there is the smell."

"Yeah," said Eric, mentally living the cheese life.

"And what, by the way, is wrong with getting the

band back together?" said Buddy, fixing his father with a level brown gaze.

"The bird," said Eric.

"What bird?"

"Some bird. There was a bird."

"Oh, come *on*," said Lou. "I mean, 'Pig Train,' you've played it five thousand times, a couple more won't hurt you."

Eric's sneaker was scuffling the floor. "Yeah," he said. "No. Like."

Enid was familiar with her employer's mysterious moods. "You embarrassed or something?" she said.

"Forgotten the words," said Eric.

"Of 'Pig Train'?" said Buddy, astounded.

"Mmm."

"They go like this," said Buddy. "'Pig Train, Pig Train, Pig Train, Pig Train.' Then there is the chorus. It goes 'Pig Train, Pig—'"

"'Train'!" said Eric, beaming.

"Give me strength," said Buddy.

"Brilliant!" cried Lou, beaming right back at her father and bestowing a warning kick on her brother's shin under the table.

"But I'll never do it with the band," said Eric.

"No?"

"No way. We was cursed into retirement."

"Cursed?"

"By a, like, raven. It gave me the Nevermore look. And it done something in my eye. And the other guys won't play again. No way."

During the silence caused by the impressive length of this speech, Eric rose, said, "Gotta lie down," opened the oven door, and climbed in. Enid went and helped him out. "Hot in there," he said.

"Try your bedroom. Upstairs, second on the right, black door with a skull on it and your name underneath. Your name being Eric," said Enid, steering him out of the room and shutting the door firmly behind him. "Well," she said when she came back. "That didn't go very well."

"No," said Buddy and Lou.

"If only Per were here," said Enid, with a heart-felt sigh. Perhaps she should have sighed more loudly. But that might have given people the impression that she was keen. That, thought Enid, would never do. Unladylike, for one thing. Bad tactics, for another. She suppressed another sigh. "Are you two here for lunch?" she said.

"Yes," said Buddy.

"No," said Lou.

"Make up your minds."

Lou looked at Buddy. Buddy looked at Lou. "No," said both of them together.

"All right, Lou," said Buddy, when Enid had sailed out of the room. "What is it?"

"What is what?" said Lou, who liked to tease her highly intelligent brother.

"They are big," said Buddy. "We are children. What can we do?"

Reverently, Lou opened her leather-bound edition of *Tales from the Brothers Grime*. It had been thrown at her by the famous cellist Stropovich when he had collected an award for playing on Death Eric's famous experimental *Cellophane Hell* album. She had treasured it ever since. "Listen to 'The Tale of the Ant and the House,'" she said. "'An ant, wishing to steal a house from a man, did elaborate handstands and other acrobatics, hoping that the man would feel inadequate and leave. When this did not work, the ant stationed itself in the man's bed. Every time the man was about to go to sleep, the ant bit him on the bum. Eventually the man jumped out of the window and ran away, leaving the house to the ant.'"

"Wha?" said Buddy.

Lou tapped the Good Book. "As you said, dear brother," she said, "they are big and we are small. Like ants. Let us go out there and do some acrobatics and, if necessary, bite some bum."

"Acrobatics?" said Buddy. Beads of sweat stood on his pale brow. Like many logical geniuses, he was really quite simpleminded.

"Let me break it down into phases for you. Phase One we could call Getting the Band Together."

"Not easy."

"Quite. Phase Two we could call Getting Them Rehearsed."

"Easier."

"Phase Three is Organizing the Tour. Phase Four is Making the New Album. Phase Five is Adjusting the Omens."

"Omens. You mean the raven," said Buddy. "I mean, how do you get a raven to hop onto a stage and say with regard to that curse issued by that other raven, 'It didn't mean it, plus I am sorry it did that in your eye,' all without talking?"

Lou shook her head. For a moment her cheerful features had a squashed look, as if weighed down by heavy cares. Then she brightened and her eyes took on the old emerald gleam. "I have a plan.

Quick! To the library!"

The library at Dunravin was a stately chamber, modeled on the one at Balmoral Castle, summer home of Her Maj the Queen of England. It was the work of a moment to heave the ancient scrapbooks from the bottom shelves and spread them on the green-leather-topped table. The yellowed pages lay before them in all their mellow splendor: *Melody Maker*, *Smash Hits*, *New Musical Express*, *Kerrangg!*, *Jackie*, *Black Leather*, and a lot of metal titles too loathsome to mention. In those great leather-bound volumes was every mention of Death Eric there had ever been in the world's press.

"All *right*," said Buddy, pink with delight now that he saw where his sister's thoughts were carrying them. "Ready when you are."

"Pencil sharp?"

"And licked."

"OK," said Lou, turning to a *Black Leather* feature called DEATH ERIC—WE ASK THE QUESTIONS, THEY TELL IT LIKE IT IS! "Phase One. Take One. Action!"

It was several months since Fingers Trubshaw had last picked up his bass guitar. Fingers did not mind.

43

Nowadays he was the managing director of a company called GFT. "GFT" stood for "Green Fingers Trubshaw," and it had interests in the horticulture and garden maintenance industries. And one employee: himself.

Dum-di-dum, a-stuttabum, stuttabum, hummed Fingers as he steered the mower across the velvet lawn of Zelda Startlepuss, the city's mayor. When he reached the end of the lawn, he turned the mower around and went back. Who said gardening was a job without much variety? You got to drive there. Then you got to drive back. Then there. Then—

"Oops," said Fingers Trubshaw, interrupting the steady bass line in his head. For there ahead of him were a girl of about twelve and a boy of about eleven, both smartly dressed in blazers, the boy pale in fashionable black, the girl in an elegant boxpleated skirt of rust red, with bright green shoes that matched her eyes. They were standing exactly where he planned to mow next. "Oi!" he said. "Clear off!"

The children put their hands in the air and waved. In their hands, Trubshaw now saw, were, like, books or something. He squinted through his gardener's safety glasses. The books both said AUTOGRAPHS.

A small feeling of smugness grew in Fingers's broad chest. He slowed, turned off the mower engine, and pushed the glasses back on his head. "Arternoon, kids," he said. "And what can I do for you?"

The children smiled smiles of sickening sweetness. "We think you're soooo cool!" cried the girl.

"You're our mum's absolute favorite!" cried the boy.

"Sign our books, please, oh do, oh you might, oh please, you're so famous!" they both cried together, jumping up and down in a frankly artificial manner.

"Yeah," said Fingers, blushing and taking the books. It was years since anything like this had happened to him. He scribbled.

"I hope your bear called Davies is in the best of health," said the girl.

"My *what*?" said Trubshaw.

"It said in a magazine we read that you had a bear called Davies, that your favorite color was purple, and your favorite food was mashed potatoes," said the boy.

"Cor!" said Fingers. "That goes back, what, twenty years? Anyway I made it all up. Never knew what silly questions them magazines were going to ask you next."

"Oh," said Buddy and Lou, for it was them. Their attempt to be nice to this stout old chap seemed to be going rather badly. The boy pulled a bag from his pocket and said, "Have one."

"What are they?" said Fingers, who now wished to get on with his mowing.

"Jelly babies," said Lou. "It says in the *New Musical Express* that they are your favorite."

"In 1985, maybe," said Fingers. "Nowadays I got to watch my weight, you know how it is. Healthy life, healthy life, don't eat sweets and stay out of strife."

"Fascinating," said Lou, meaning exactly the opposite. "So you don't like custard, are not Aquarius, and are not looking for a girl who will have your babies and look after the vegetable garden."

"Correct," said Trubshaw. "Now, nice as this is, I've got a lot of stripes to put on a lot of lawns—"

"So if we said that we are longing for you to put the band back together again, would you be interested?"

"Interested?" Trubshaw laughed heartily, sending pigeons clattering off a nearby patch of cabbages. "Definitely not."

"But what about your fans?" said Buddy.

Trubshaw wiped away a fake tear of sympathy. He thought of patting Buddy on the head, but there was a look in the child's dark and intelligent eye that made him think this would not be advisable, plus there was the hair gel. "I've got a business, sonny," he said. He waved an arm at the velvet lawns stretching in all directions. "My patch. My vocation," he said. "See that shed over there? Got eight mowers in there, coarse, coarse medium, medium medium, fine, superfine, double superfine, cutthroat razor and a spare. Plus thousands of gallons of the best weed killer and other fine lawn chemicals, needing to be applied with skill for optimum results. I've got a fortune tied up in this business, dozens of clients who rely on me. I couldn't let them down."

"So," said Buddy, with the air of one solving an equation. "If you didn't have any machines and you didn't have any clients—"

"I'd go back to rock 'n' roll," said Fingers Trubshaw, laughing heartily at the impossibility of the idea.

"Promise?" said Lou, breathless with hope.

"Ho, ho, ho," said Fingers, pocketing the card Lou gave him without looking at it. "Of course I promise. Now stand clear!"

The mower started. Off he went down the stripe. *Bombappa bombappa bip* boom *di,* said the bass line between his ears. He wagged his head, grinning.

Kids!

Kenyatta McClatter was parked in his usual spot by the war memorial in the town square. Everything was as it should be. The fat in the fryers was at exactly 385° Fahrenheit. The chips were cut three inches long, a half an inch thick. The fish was ready for battering in special batter, lined up in rhythmic rows: cod, skate, conger, snapper, ling, salmon, saveloys, Mars bars, African fry pie. Kenyatta McClatter stood with his tam-o'-shanter square on his mighty Afro, his eyes gleaming in his dark brown skin, the chicken drumsticks in his hands playing drumbeats on the fryer lids: *a-reebap, areebap, a bippety bap* bap. He looked exactly like a Scottish fish-frying drummer of Kenyan extraction. This was not amazing, because that is exactly what he was.

At five to five he shoveled a bundle of chips into the fryer. The world vanished in a cloud of steam.

48

When the steam cleared, two children were standing in front of the van.

"Not ready yet," said Kenyatta McClatter.

"We don't want chips," said the green-eyed girl, who was, of course, Lou.

"We would very much like your autograph, though," said the boy in black, who was, of course, Buddy.

"And why," said Kenyatta McClatter, "would you be wanting the autograph of a humble Scottish fish fryer?"

From behind the little girl's back appeared a large leather-bound book. "You were not always as we see you now," she said.

"Meaning?"

"It says here in *NME* that your greatest ambition is to walk on the moon," said Buddy, looking dark and judicious. "I respect that."

"Been there," said Kenyatta. "Done that."

"And that your second dearest wish is to skateboard down Mount Kenya."

"Done that too," said McClatter.

"The moon and Mount Kenya are one thing," said Lou, a challenging glint in her green eyes. "But playing music is something you never finish."

"Wha?" said McClatter, who had no idea what she was talking about.

"You played drums in Death Eric," said Lou. "Don't you miss it?"

"I play drums anywhere," said McClatter, the chicken bones going *a-rittlibip, a-reebap, areebap* bim. "I liked playing with Death Eric. But not as much as I like playing in my van. In my van, see, I can play drums and sell fish and chips too. On one of those stages in front of, say, half a million people, there is no fryer for fish frying, so I feel I am not realizing my full potential. See what I mean?"

"So if I was to say we are your greatest fans ever and we are re-forming the band?"

"I'd say good luck to you," said McClatter. "You'll need it. And you'd be doing it without me. I like fish frying," he said. "It's steady."

"So far," said Buddy, with a small and rather worrying smile. "May we leave our card?"

"Sure. Now if you will excuse me," said McClatter, tucking the card away in his apron without looking at it and giving a final drumbeat, "these chips is done, and here comes me public."

*

"Hmm," said Lou. "Acrobatics have failed. The Brothers Grime say they always do."

"So we must conclude," said Buddy, with the air of one who has weighed things up, "that it is time to bite bum."

The next day was bright and sunny. *Doom doom doom doom*, hummed Fingers Trubshaw as he cycled toward the shed that held the Green Fingers Trubshaw mower fleet. As Fingers came to the top of the hill, he was humming an important twiddly bit, or fill, as bassists call them.

The gardens he looked after lay in a great bowl of ground, with the mower shed at its center. He loved cresting the rise and seeing the bowl spread before him, studded with the stately homes of his clients like jewels in the green velvet of the lawns.

Not this morning.

The fill died on his lips. This morning, the bowl was a five-mile disk of dirty brown. Fingers Trubshaw clutched his hair. He said, "Weed killer."

In the middle of the brown bowl, his shed still stood. Squinting, he had the idea that the door was swinging open, as if it had been broken into. But before he could confirm this, the shed bulged at the sides and grew an attractive orange rose of flame. *Boom*, said the explosion a little later. Fiery fragments of lawn mower shot in all directions. One especially hot lump landed on the mayor's roof, which caught fire.

Fingers Trubshaw was beyond speech. If he had been able to speak, he would have said "Ooer," or possibly "Whoops." His career was in ruins, and judging by the ghastly destruction down there, the police would soon be after him as well.

Dimly, he remembered those kids.

His trembling fingers went to the pocket of his tweed waistcoat and pulled out the card they had left the day before. He read it. His eyes became narrow and calculating. He needed to be somewhere safe, protected by giant roadies.

Dunravin would do nicely.

At ten to five that afternoon, Kenyatta McClatter was cutting up his chips in the van, talking to his friend Alphonse Quing, the Sanitary Inspector. Alphonse was cruel but fair. He had been known to shut down a café because of a speck of dust on a waiter's shoe. But he had never found anything to raise one of his thin eyebrows at in Kenyatta's van. Scrupulously clean was what it was, if you asked him. And in accordance with all hygiene regulations. Alphonse Quing could think of no higher praise. He had once described his dear son Arthur as "quite clean," at which point Arthur had burst into tears of joy and had to be given sips of distilled water to calm him down. Get the picture? Bit of a stickler, Alphonse Quing.

So imagine the surprise of Inspector Quing when he noticed behind Kenyatta McClatter's back, sitting on its hind legs and gnawing a raw chip, a large black rat.

Quing slid smoothly into Avenging Angel mode. "I have to report a rodent on the wipe-clean surface," he said. "This is very serious."

"Ho, ho, you funnin' me, pal," said Kenyatta, turning. Then he cried, "Aieeee!" and hurled a dishcloth. The rat leaped into the deep-fat fryer, hissed and was no more. "Whoa!" said Kenyatta. "I'll change the lard."

"Not so fast," said Quing, his eyes now narrow, his nostrils twitching at the hot scent of fried rat and Regulations Defied. "By the authority vested in me by the council, I am sealing this facility pending search!"

"Oi!" cried Kenyatta.

Too late. Quing had entered the van through the back door and was going through the lockers, in which he discovered the following: two live rats, one dead ditto, one large handful of cockroaches, one lump raw horsemeat with the skin on, and four frozen gerbils. Inspection of the fridge revealed a big coiled reptile, apparently of the python family, which was not approached, due to operative health and safety considerations, like it was hissing a bit and gnashing its fangs.

"*Well,*" said Quing, straightening up, opening his notebook, and licking his pencil. "In all my career, I have never seen the like. They are going to lock you up, Mr. McClatter, and throw away the key. Of course, our personal friendship has hitherto been a warm one, but it is more than my job's worth to—hey!"

For Kenyatta McClatter was no longer in the van. The square rang to the *bip-bap a-reebap* rhythm of his boots as he thundered into the mean streets of the town. In a dark alley, he wiped his steamy brow with his Balmoral hat. His trembling fingers went to the pocket of his apron and hauled out the card the kid had given him the day before. He read it. His eyes grew large and round. Personal fulfillment was one thing. Spending the rest of his life in jail was another. He needed to be somewhere safe, protected by giant roadies.

Dunravin would do nicely.

Buddy and Lou were in their dayroom above the front door as Kenyatta's bicycle screeched around the gatepost and skidded to a halt by the portico.

"Mission accomplished," said Lou, looking up from her book. "Your rats did not die in vain."

"They died in van," said Buddy, finishing the calculation on which he had been working.

"Ha ha," said Lou politely. "Shall we move on to the next phase?"

"Of course," said Buddy.

Lou bowed her head. This evening's plan was not covered by the Brothers Grime. It was the invention of her brother, Buddy, and therefore just as subtle and nearly as good.

Down the stairs they went. From the kitchen came the sound of backs being slapped and glass breaking.

"They're bonding," said Lou.

The scene around the kitchen table was indeed a merry one. Eric was beaming. He had removed the corks from several bottles of champagne and handed them out. The band members and roadies were hosing each other down with fizz, to the accompaniment of cries of joy and mighty guffaws. Flatpick the budgie was swearing horribly in his cage.

"Hey!" shouted Eric, when his eye stumbled on his children. "The band's back together!"

"Fancy that," said Lou, stepping to one side to avoid a jet of champagne.

Buddy caught Enid's eye and raised one dark eyebrow a fraction. She galumphed over and put an arm around his shoulder. "Have you fixed the you-know-whats?" he said.

"Trust me."

Suzuki's Law states that at rock-and-roll band reunions, someone will suggest a few rounds on the quad bike course out back. But it doesn't always happen.

"Hey!" said Eric. "I know! What about a bit of quad bike, like, action?"

"Arriiight!" cried one and all.

Out they piled into the summer evening. The

mighty steeds were lined up in anticipation. Leaping aboard, the metal warriors gunned the engines. But instead of shooting off like guided missiles, the bikes trundled briskly but safely toward the ramps and hollows of the course.

"Oi!" cried Fingers. "This is rubbish! They won't go!"

"You're doing sixty-five, dearie," said Enid, fingers crossed behind her back. "But your reflexes are so good, it seems slower."

"I'm a rider at the gates of Hell and I take no prisoners!" cried Eric, trundling along the track.

"Me too!" roared Trubshaw.

"And me!" cried Kenyatta.

"Yee ha!" cried Eric, beetling very slowly down a muddy slope.

"Yee ha!" cried Kenyatta and Fingers, beetling after him.

Enid watched the departing silhouettes. "Aaah," she said. "Look at 'em, bless their hearts."

"Do you think it will work?" said Buddy.

Enid stood with her vast arms folded under her floral-print bosom and said nothing. There was a worried look on her enormous face.

"She doesn't think it will," said Buddy.

Enid patted him absentmindedly on the head, stunning him slightly. "Per would know," said Enid.

"He's sure to be back soon," said Buddy.

"He always is," said Lou.

Enid gave them a kind smile, and so did the skull tattooed on her kneecap. But Lou thought that the great rolling landscape of her face seemed shadowed, as if by the threat of storms, and Buddy thought she looked worried. Which in the end amounted to the same thing.

3

There was a lot of bread thrown at supper that night, followed by a custard fight, followed by some high jinks involving fire extinguishers. Eventually, Enid, Lou, and Buddy had had enough.

"All right," said Enid, as BB the roadie swept up broken glass. "It's four o'clock in the morning. Bedtime."

"Aaaah," moaned Kenyatta. "I was just gettin' into it."

"Yeah," said Fingers. "I'd forgotten how cool it was, rock and roll, like."

"Rock and ROLL!" cried the three grown men, making peace signs and fist salutes.

Lou and Buddy, already horribly overtired, found themselves suddenly horribly embarrassed as well.

"Get a good night's sleep," said Enid. "Because tomorrow we are going to start practicing bright and early at four thirty in the afternoon. OK?"

"'Spose," said the rockers, and they mooched off to bed.

Next morning a policeman came around, searching for the person who had burned down the mayor's house and the worst food hygiene offender since records began.

"Sorry, officer," said Enid, looking up as she poured tea for Lou and Buddy. "Can't help you there. Would you like some CDs?"

"Autographed by Death Eric?" said the policeman, going pink. "He's a hero of mine."

"Obviously." Enid handed over a *Greatest Hits* boxed set. "Now run along, shoo."

"Sorry you was *mmf*," said the policeman as Enid shut the door in his face.

"OK," said Buddy, frowning at the interruption. "We must get them to practice."

"How?" said Lou. "Bonding is fun. Practicing is work. They hate work."

"They've just got to," said Buddy. "It's part of the Plan. They want to succeed again. So it's in their interest."

"Sometimes," said Lou, sighing, "you think like a machine, not a person."

"We have to put them under pressure," said Buddy, his face dark and faraway.

"Such as?" said Lou.

"I'm going to call Mum."

"*Ulp*," said Lou, paling. "Are you sure?"

Buddy was already dialing.

Lou watched him with an anxious face. Enid put a large, hard hand on hers. Lou felt herself relax. Enid was so comforting. Much more comforting than—

"Mrs. Wave Thrashmettle," said Buddy into the telephone. "Please."

He listened. He said, "Oh." He hung up the phone. He stared at the table in front of him.

"Well?" said Lou, with an attempt at hope.

"That was her assistant," said Buddy in a flat,

disappointed voice. "She is doing Levitation in the Room with the Padded Ceiling. She cannot be disturbed for six days for fear of a crash landing. Apparently she thinks that yoga is more important than children. She has been talking to Dad on the phone. She says it would be bad karma to try to persuade him to do anything he does not want to do. She is of the opinion that the Curse of the Raven must be dealt with on the astral plane. She is sending Sid the Soothsayer on a special course."

"I'll tell him," said Enid.

There was a long, gloomy silence of the kind often associated with Wave Thrashmettle, whether she was at home or far away. Enid put her hands on the table, palm up. Buddy gave her his long, inky fingers. Lou gave her her pink, pointed fingers. Enid squeezed affectionately. They squeezed back.

"No practicing means no more scientific instruments," said Buddy.

"No more clothes. No more house."

Silence fell; a thick silence, heavy with one terrible thought.

Enid might behave like a huge, tough extra

mother. But she was on wages. And if there was no money to pay her wages . . .

Buddy looked at Enid. Lou looked at Enid. Enid went pink.

"Ahem," she said, clearing her throat. "It is true that a girl has to make a living and I have received an attractive offer from Big Mabel's Lady Wrestler Circus. But children"—she squeezed their hands again, this time carried away by her feelings—"I will stay with you for as long as humanly possible, and we will work this out."

"Dear Enid!" cried Lou faintly, massaging her squashed fingers.

"The first thing to do," said Buddy, clenching and unclenching his hand to make sure it still worked, "is to make them practice. Then, when Per turns up, he can take over."

"Quite so," said Enid grimly. She still adored Per, but there was beginning to be quite a lot of questions she wanted to ask him.

After the conference with Enid, the children took mugs of tea upstairs to the Men of Metal.

Lou took Kenyatta his. "Big day today," she said. "Practice day."

Kenyatta groaned. He had a bad headache. "I've been thinking," he said. "Maybe I better go back, clean up my van, explain—"

"Too late," said Lou grimly. "The police have already been around. You're the Adolf Hitler of kitchen hygiene. Stray too far from a roadie, you're toast."

"Oh *no*," said Kenyatta, pushing the tea away from him like a man who has lost the will to live.

"But there's an old drum kit of yours in the cellar."

"Hooray," said Kenyatta glumly.

But Lou noticed that he sat up in bed and started to drink his tea.

Buddy took Fingers his. "Lot to do," he said. "Sleep well?"

Fingers groaned. He had a bad headache. "I dunno," he said. "I think I'd better go and see my clients. I could always say I wanted to reseed their lawns. And as for the mowers, I could rebuild—"

"The police were here," said Buddy grimly. "You're wanted for arson and lawn murder. If you go anywhere without a roadie, someone will lock you up and throw the key into an active volcano."

"Oh *no*," said Fingers, pushing his tea away from him like a man who has lost the will to live.

"But there's a bass amp and one of your old guitars in the cellar," said Buddy.

"Great," said Fingers glumly.

But Buddy noticed that he sat up in bed and started to drink his tea.

The children took the last mug of tea up to their dad. The bed had not been slept in. They found him dozing on the windowsill, his vampire bat, Dave, upside down on the curtain above him. "Tea," said the kids.

"Nice," said Eric, waking with a start and falling off the windowsill. "What we doin' today, eh?"

"Practicing," said the children, like one child.

"I dunno," said Eric.

"What don't you know?"

"'Ever since . . . you know."

"That raven looked at you?" Lou arched a cynical eyebrow.

"Don't mention ravens!"

"No croaking egg-laying animal with big black wings, then, can cause you any trouble in the rehearsal studio."

"Yeah," said Eric. His eyebrows came together.

His jaw swung free. "What were we talkin' about?"

"You are going to play the guitar while Fingers plays bass and Kenyatta plays drums."

"Yeah," said Eric. He did not sound enthusiastic.

But the children noticed that he sat up on the floor and drank his tea.

The rehearsal room at Dunravin had been built as a bunker against alien attack by the house's first owner. It was reached by a spiral staircase a hundred feet deep, tiled with alien recognition charts in bright mosaic.

All day long the roadies had toiled to get the gear down the stairs. They had set it up exactly as in the old days. Kenyatta's kit was in the middle, cymbals like flying saucers orbiting the space city of the drums. To Kenyatta's left stood the bass stack, six and a half feet high, a row of red and green lights winking from the control panel. In front of the stack, glowing red-hot in the spotlight, was a flame-red Fender Precision bass guitar. On the other side of the drums were four huge Marshall speakers and amplifiers, except that roadies do not call them speakers and amplifiers but cabinets and tops, and, reader, we will follow their example.

From the tops, leads ran to a huge red neon-lit pedal that said TREAD HERE, ERIC. On the stand by the pedal stood Eric's legendary guitar, Rabid Dingo—a night-black Gibson Flying V, filthy dirty and covered in toothmarks.

Buddy and Lou surveyed the scene, shaking their heads. Lou thought longingly of her book, her cello under the domed ceiling of the Blue Room. How heavenly it would be to read a little, then play, say, Planck's *Teatime Interlude* with Buddy. Buddy looked at the gear and found it weirdly old-fashioned. He longed to rebuild it; or, failing that, to retreat to the Blue Room and let his fingers run across the keyboard of the grand piano, to revel in the cool logic of, say, Planck's *Teatime Interlude* with Lou.

The two children looked at each other.

"Brace yourself," said Lou, sticking in earplugs.

"Same to you," said Buddy, gritting his teeth.

The band stepped out of the staircase and stood solemnly for a moment. This was the gear that had made them legends from Oslo to Oshawa, Penzance to Penang. Then they strolled forward and took up their positions.

At least, Fingers and Kenyatta did. Eric

wandered around the room, peering behind chairs and into speaker cabinets.

"What is it?" said Lou, who was in the control room. "Are you looking for the—"

"DON'T MENTION THE RAVEN!" roared Eric.

"Didn't," said Buddy.

Finally Eric decided that there was a complete absence of ravens. His furrowed brow cleared. Kenyatta took up a pair of sticks and rattled around the kit with a sound like a cloud thinking about thunder, *a-rippity bomp a reebop, a reebop, a* ching, then settled down to a light, tasty shuffle, like a particularly well-tuned diesel engine. Behind the pane of glass in the control room, Lou looked at Buddy and Buddy looked at Lou. Each noticed (to his or her amazement) that the other's foot was tapping.

Fingers picked up the bass and ducked through the strap. He reached up a finger and flicked the STANDBY switch to ON. He wedged his right thumb against the thumb rest. His fingers went out and touched a string. *DUMMM*, said the bass, smack on the beat. Kenyatta's groove flowed up through the soles of Fingers's feet and into his hands. *Bapa*

68

dum bit, bibi dum bit, dummity dum a reebop, said the bass, weaving round Kenyatta's bass drum to make the diesel rhythm into a big truck rhythm, all the parts working together.

Behind the pane of glass in the control room, Lou looked at Buddy and Buddy looked at Lou. Each was astonished to see that the other's left foot was still tapping, and so was the right foot, and the fingers were beating out a *dippity dappity doo dah* rhythm on the mixing board.

Eric shuffled uncertainly toward his band. He was wearing a black singlet that came down to his knees. His black jeans flopped down over his sneakers. His nose stuck out of the green curtains of hair like a lump of chalk, and a bat fluttered around his head. He snapped his fingers restlessly and tripped over a couple of leads. He picked up Rabid Dingo and strapped it to his body and looked for the controls and the strings. He could not find them. A junior under-assistant roadie trotted out of the control room, carefully moved Eric's hands away, unstrapped the guitar, turned it around so the strings faced outward instead of into Eric's singlet, and strapped it reverently on again. Eric did not even look down. His eyes went up to the Marshall top, checked the controls, and saw that they were good. He pulled the 10mm plectrum from under the Baron Samedi souvenir of Haiti human ear plectrum holder on Rabid Dingo's gnawed tailfin. He switched on all five pickups, full treble the front two, full bass the back three. The side of his hand wiped the volume control to 11. His sneaker moved along the floor like a questing skunk. It found the pedal. It stood on the pedal. The plectrum (which guitar players call a pick, so from now on, reader, so shall we) rose. The fingers of the left hand hung a moment, poised. *A whee bam, a whee bam, a whibbidy bibbidy seebam*, went the rhythm section.

Eric Thrashmettle's fingers hit the frets. Eric Thrashmettle's pick hit the strings.

Somewhere in the stack, a 750cc motorcycle started up, accelerated to 130 mph in first gear, and drove into a plate-glass bus full of angels, who screamed in perfect harmony and joined a flock of migrating devil bats heading for the back door of Hell.

Behind the pane of glass in the control room, Lou looked with amazement at Buddy and Buddy looked with amazement at Lou. This amazement was because each noticed that the other's feet were still tapping, and that the other's fingers were still beating out a *dippity dappity doo dah* rhythm on the mixing desk. Each also noticed that the other's hair was standing on end, and that the head was beginning to nod. In no time at all, the nod had become a jerk, and the jerk a full-scale bang.

Unbelievable, thought Lou. Thirty bars ago, my dear brother and I were despising feedback metal and yearning for the chilly tinklings of Planck. Now we're both headbanging, and we can't help ourselves—

But Buddy's head, fingers, and feet had become still. His supermusical ear had caught the faintest hint of something off. And all of a sudden, the great metal juggernaut in the rehearsal room was an ordinary truck and the mudguards dropped off and the engine faltered and it ground to a halt and fell to bits.

"Wha?" said Eric, and he started hunting around for ravens.

"You lost it," said Fingers to Kenyatta, looking sulky.

"*You* lost it," said Kenyatta to Fingers, looking sulky himself.

"Lost what?" said Eric, still hunting.

"Nothing. The groove."

"Oh," said Eric. Definitely no ravens. "Start again?"

"Dunno," said Fingers.

"What?"

"'S not right," said Fingers.

"Know what you mean," said Kenyatta.

Eric was rummaging under his singlet, his green hair swinging in a dazed manner. He pulled out a bat and threw it away. He said, "What's wrong?"

"'S nothing," said Fingers. "Doesn't feel right."

"'S got to be something."

"Dunno," said Kenyatta. "Feels . . . wrong."

"This is where Per comes in," said Lou, in their corner of the control room. "Or Enid."

"And neither of them is here?"

"Enid's gone to look for Per. Didn't say when she'd be back."

Buddy's dark eyes met hers, firm and full of resolve. "It's up to us," he said.

"Quite," said Lou. She unbuttoned the special pocket in her blazer and pulled out her copy of *Tales from the Brothers Grime*. "May I remind you," she said, "of 'The Tale of Sir Chickenboy and the Lairy Godmother'?"

"Oh, pur*lease*," said Buddy. "Not the *Brothers*."

Lou ignored him, turning her green gaze upon the page. Her brother's natural curiosity would bring him around. She said, "The story concerns cowardice, ingratitude, and the restoration of confidence by familiar objects."

"'Zat so?" said Buddy, dead sarcastic.

"'Once upon a time,'" said Lou, sighing, "'there was a child called Brutus. He had a godmother who was lairy, which means she used to nick stuff. Well, Brutus's fairy godmother had given him a shocking-pink nylon teddy bear and his lairy godmother took a strong fancy to it. So she nicked Brutus's teddy out of the crib.'"

"And?" said Buddy.

"'After the theft of the bear Brutus changed. He had been a tough little mite, full of grins and punches. Now he began to wet the bed and whimper. His parents changed his name to Chickenboy, and gave up on him.

"'In later life, he was challenged to a duel by a tough guy called Sir Beefcake. Sir Beefcake had, weirdly enough, inherited a pink bear from a little old lady who was actually none other than the lairy godmother. He used the bear as a mascot and stuck it on his helmet.

"'Seeing his lost treasure on his enemy's hat, Chickenboy's terror turned instantly to rage. He wrenched the stuffed beast from its moorings. Then he struck Beefcake a fierce blow with his mace and married a princess who had been watching and had been most impressed. Needless to say, they lived happily ever after.'"

"Fascinating," said Buddy. "Pardon my asking, but so what?"

"Fingers and Kenyatta are missing their favorite things," said Lou. "Like you miss that smelly old bit of blanket you used to sniff all the time—"

"Oh. Yeah. Right," said Buddy hastily.

Lou smiled sweetly at her brother. "I knew you would understand," she said. "Now, we need to give them a lawn mower and a fish fryer and bring them out of the bunker into a familiar world. Death Eric *will* be brilliant."

"All right," said Buddy, crisp and efficient. "Is there a phone down here?"

"Over there. Why?"

"Because I am right now going to get on it and start bending the vicar's ear about hiring the village hall."

*

It worked.

At the sight of the 2,500cc Wheel Horse Professional Lawn Mower parked by the village hall, Fingers Trubshaw became visibly calmer. His face turned an enthusiastic pink, and he undid several of the buttons of his tweed waistcoat. Kenyatta walked twitchily into the hall and stopped as if shot. Over the drum kit was hung a great banner on which were painted in psychedelic script the words FRYING TONITE. His fish and potatoes were neatly laid out on a table behind the drums. And to one side of the floor tom-toms stood a fifty-five-gallon oil barrel in which forty-five gallons of the best lard were coming to a boil over a gas ring.

A tear rolled down Kenyatta McClatter's chocolate cheek. "You shouldn't have," he said, walking toward his lard like a man in a beautiful dream.

"Let's see if you can cut it," said Buddy.

McClatter whipped out his knife. He gutted and boned a cod, sliced it into fillets, battered it thoroughly, and tossed it neatly into the lard. "See?" he said, over the hiss.

"You're really cookin'," said Buddy.

But Kenyatta was not listening. Humming a little tune, he was chipping potatoes and laying out vinegar and salt on white paper towels spread over the bass speakers. Buddy was impressed. Kenyatta really had his chips together.

Having taken in the happy scene in the hall, Lou went outside again to talk to Fingers Trubshaw about his new mower.

But Fingers was gone.

All that remained was a slight pall of blue exhaust, and the clatter of a 2,500cc Wheel Horse Professional from the summer day outside.

Lou headed for the door.

In front of the hall was a patch of manky grass with a couple of picnic tables on it. Fingers had directed some roadies to move the tables. Now he was on his tweed knees, shaking his head.

"Can I help?" said Lou, assuming the poor oaf was having some kind of fit.

"Highly doubtful," said Fingers. "We're, like, doomed. You've got your burrowing insects, your mold, your moss, and your mineral deficiencies. To be blunt, this lawn is on the critical list. It needs, let me see, six weeks' intensive care. Not cheap, neither. Fertilize, aerate, scarify—"

Lou felt she might nod off at any moment, but she could not help identifying with the bassist's obvious pain. She said, "Why not give it a mow, for starters, and then play some bass?"

Fingers sucked air through his teeth. "I dunno," he said.

"Oops," said Lou, looking at her watch. "I've got to go to the police now."

"Wha?"

"To help them with their inquiries into arson and—"

"Ten minutes," said Trubshaw, white as a sheet.

"Eight," said Buddy, appearing at the door and setting the stopwatch bezel on his Rolex.

"I'll be there."

"Now," said Lou, when the bassist was safely mowing, "where's Dad?"

"Usual thing, I should think," said Buddy.

The two rock-and-roll children strolled over to the village hall lavatories.

"Dad?" they said.

"Thank God you've come," said the familiar voice from within the cubicle.

"You stuck?"

"Certainly am."

Lou said, "So—"

"Leave this to me," said Buddy.

Lou nodded. She always deferred to her brother on technical questions.

"Now then," he said, "put your hand on the door. Run it down. See the little thing on the side of the door?"

"'S dark in here."

"Use your fingers."

"Yeah."

"It's a bolt."

"No, 's not. 'S a hinge."

"Try the other side of the door."

Fumblings came from within.

"There's a handle. Pull it back. It's a bolt. You'll be able to get out."

"Don't wanna."

"*What?*"

"'S safe in here."

Lou sensed that it was time for some input from her. She said in a kindly voice, "It's safe out here too."

"No, 's not."

"What," said Lou soothingly, "is the problem?"

"Look up," said Eric.

Lou and Buddy looked up. There was a large oak tree by the village hall.

"There's a tree," they said.

"And in the tree?"

The branches were full of big, untidy nests. Black birds hopped and flapped, cawing.

"That like raven," said Eric, "he's sent the brothers. Well, that's it. The curse is still in force. I retire."

"They are rooks," said Buddy. "Members of the crow family, certainly. But *Corvus frugilegus*, not *Corvus corax*. Quite different."

"Wha?"

"Not ravens," said Lou, realizing that Buddy was going right over his father's head. "Totally not ravens. Come out, and we'll hide you."

"Oh." Fumbling noises came from the lav. Out slunk Eric. His children wrapped him in a cloak and smuggled him into the hall.

Buddy looked at his Rolex. "Two minutes," he said.

"Chips, anyone?" said Kenyatta McClatter.

The rehearsal started greasily, but exactly on time. The music was . . . well.

Buddy and Lou sat in comfortable swivel chairs behind the mixing desk. Their right feet tapped as one right foot. Buddy watched Lou's head. Lou watched Buddy's head. The number under rehearsal was "Pass the Chainsaw When You've Finished with the Donkey, George." Judging by early videos, audience heads had once banged practically off when Eric played "Donkey." But Buddy saw no bang to Lou's head, and Lou detected not the merest trace of a nod in her brother. Buddy watched Kenyatta wait for a stop in the song, get up, walk over to the lard vat, try a chip, and adjust the gas. Fingers, meanwhile, was craning out of the window to make sure that nobody had pinched the mower. And Eric himself was casting nervous glances at the treeful of rooks. It was no wonder that when it was time to come in after the stop, they came in raggedly.

"Nooo!" cried Eric, stamping on the pedal and hitting a mighty power chord.

The music ceased.

But not the sound.

Things were falling on the roof—large, heavy things. There was also the sound of voices, raised in not very enthusiastic shouts. A window broke and a brickbat landed on the floor. Tied to the brickbat was a label that said HUSH. Someone started battering on the door. BB the roadie picked up a fire extinguisher, ripped off the safety catch, and started striding toward the interruption.

"Wait!" said Lou. BB stopped in midstride. "No violence!"

"Wha?" said BB.

"Discussion is better," said Buddy. "Leave it to Lou."

Lou pasted a sweet, merry smile on her face. She went to the door and opened it. A couple of dozen Costa de Lott residents in expensive leisurewear were milling outside, shouting and waving tennis rackets. Lou recognized a top chef and a duchess. She was pretty sure she had seen the rest of them on TV and in magazines.

"Welcome!" she cried.

"What?" cried the residents.

There was a slight commotion. A man in a black robe pushed to the front.

"Afternoon, Vicar!" said Lou.

"Erm, we've come to sort of raise an issue about the noise," said the vicar. "It's too much, that is to say, a little, er, audible."

"It panicked my chihuahua!" cried a blond actress in leopardskin Lycra.

"It put me off my drop shot!" cried last year's Worplesdon champion.

"And it isn't as if the music's any good!" cried the Leader of the Opposition.

"Jejune!"

"Derivative!"

"You are talking," said Lou, "about *Death Eric*."

There was a silence.

"Not *the* Death Eric?" said someone.

"The one and only."

"Cor."

More silence.

"And now," said Lou, "Death Eric is proud to invite you into the village hall you have hospitably rented to the band for quite a lot of money. Once inside, all residents will be provided with free cod and chips plus a lecture on lawn care from one of the country's premier experts."

"Fish and chips," went the murmur. "Lawn care. Gosh. Awfully tempting."

Murmuring enthusiastically, the residents crowded in.

Twenty minutes later, Kenyatta's oil drum was empty except for the lard and the odd floating chip. Fingers Trubshaw had discussed lawn enemies such as moss, clover, and the wee of lady dogs. Eric had just about got his guitar in tune. And back at the mixing board, the children were taking charge.

"Right!" cried Lou, as the applause for the lawn lecture died away and Buddy set the levels. "The lads will now play a short set. You're welcome to stay, residents!"

"How lovely!" they cried.

Buddy punched a button.

"When you're ready, Dad!" cried Lou.

Off they went.

At first, the residents stood around, shaking their heads. Then they seemed to prick up their ears. A Panama hat twitched on the right-hand side of the hall under the British Legion banner. A thousand-pound hairdo jerked on the left-hand side of the hall under the WI Tea Things Rota.

"Banging," said Lou, trying to hide her excitement.

Buddy frowned, bent over the mixing board. As always, he was inclined to be skeptical. But after a while, he had to admit that his sister was right. Hairdos and Panamas were banging. Soothed with chips and lawns and the absence of ravens, Death Eric was playing a bit of a blinder.

In a village hall. To twenty-one posh people and

a Borzoi. It might be music, but it was a long way from a comeback tour.

"Like to try mixing?" said Lou to BB.

"Love to," said BB, blushing.

"All yours," said Lou. "Buddy, outside."

They sat on a bench by the village green.

Lou said, "How does a tour work?"

"Totally straightforward," said Buddy. "You get a fleet of lorries, a few limos, load up the gear and the people, and off you go."

"Off you go where?"

"The venues. The hotels."

"And who finds the venues?"

"They're on the contracts."

"And who makes the contracts?"

There was a pause. Then both at once they said, "Per."

"Per'll turn up," said Lou.

"Of course he will," said Buddy.

There was another pause, longer.

Buddy said, "I'm going to ring Enid." He dialed.

"Hello, love," said Enid's voice.

Buddy could feel Lou's green eyes burning into his. "We were just wondering if you had had a chance to talk to Per," he said.

More silence. "Not as such," said Enid in a slightly strangled voice, as if she had to say something she did not want to say. "But I heard *of* him."

"And?"

"I got a call from Ronnie the Roller, car dealer by appointment to your old man and other rock royalty. Weekly courtesy call, are we all right for Aston Martins and similar. And do you know what he was saying?"

"*Obviously* not," said Buddy, with a sharpness he instantly regretted.

"Sorry, love," said Enid, who had heard worse. "Well, what he was saying was that Per Spire went in last week and bought a matched pair of top o' the line Lamboraris. With cash, of course."

"Of course," said Buddy, lifting the phone from his ear so Lou could hear too. "Are Lamboraris expensive?"

"Just a tiny bit," said Enid.

"So they're obviously worth having, so of course Per wants some."

"No," said Enid. "Per gets ten percent of everything the band gets. So if the band is getting nothing, Per is getting ten percent of nothing. Which is?"

"Nothing," said Buddy, ever the mathematician.

"So where does the money come from for his Lamboraris?"

"Perhaps he has savings," said Lou.

"Perhaps I am a woolly rhino called Arthur," said Enid, her voice now so strangled as to be difficult to hear properly. She was talking of the man she loved, and she did not like the things she was saying.

"It is no good sitting around wondering about things," said Buddy. His mind felt as keen as a red-hot buzzsaw passing through a slab of butter. "We'll find Per, obviously, and he will explain—he always does. Meanwhile, we must get on with things. Now, where is a good place to start a tour?"

"Henge Festival, obviously," said Enid.

"Well, come back here and we'll go and talk to someone about playing there."

"You'll be lucky," said Enid.

"We are," said Lou. "We are."

4

Morrie Steam was a tall man, plump, pink, and exquisitely dressed. His cavalry-twill trousers bore razor-sharp creases and his brown brogues gleamed with a deep, soft luster. He sipped tea from an exquisite china cup and gazed doe-eyed across the great bowl of ground that was his, all his.

Once, Morrie Steam had run Yorkshire's filthiest scrapyard. He had worn steel-capped boots with the steel showing and a raincoat done up with string. He had got up at four in the morning and unscrewed carburetors and lived on the manky tomatoes he planted in the soggy driver's seats of Ford Sierras. He had driven knackered breakdown trucks in the pouring rain and come home covered in mud and engine oil and turned on the bath and discovered that there was no hot water on account of the boiler was as knackered as the breakdown truck. Then he had discovered that the derelict buses in his scrapper could quite easily be rented to hippies. Before he knew what was happening, someone had put up a stage there and bulldozed away a few Sierras, and bands were playing. He put a fence around it and charged admission. Soon he was taking as much money on the gate as he would have made out of scrap in a million years. The first thing he did after he had got rid of the last Sierra was to get the boiler mended and have a long, hot bath. The second thing was to get himself some really smart country clothes. And the third thing was to get a reputation as the meanest rock festival promoter on the planet.

He finished his tea, signed a couple of letters refusing charitable donations to orphanages, and went to look at himself in the mirror. His smooth pink face stretched away in all directions.

Maaarvellous, he thought; though there was a hair out of place . . .

There was a huge crash in the room behind him. He turned. The door was hanging off its hinges. A huge, beautiful woman with tattooed knees showing below the skirt of her print dress was standing next to two well-dressed children, brushing splinters off their blazers in a motherly fashion.

"How did you get in?" he said.

"Walked," said the wide woman, ripping the backing off a nicotine patch and slapping it on above her right knee.

Now that Morrie came to look, he observed that Neville, his chief bodyguard, seemed to be bound hand and foot and hanging from the coat peg in the anteroom by the loop in his anorak. Morrie walked carefully around his desk and sat down in the chair, thereby putting himself on the same level as the children. Buddy and Lou gave him a steady look. Morrie was a cool guy, but those green eyes acted on his soul like a blowtorch acts on a rose petal.

"Wha?" he said.

"Our dad is Eric," said Buddy.

"As in Death Eric," said Lou. "You'd like him to play at the Henge Festival."

"I—"

"At a special rate," said Lou.

"Extra special," said Buddy. "Very high."

"How much?" said Morrie.

"We will do it like this," said Buddy, reaching over the desk and laying a contract in front of Morrie. "You sign this."

Morrie cast his eye over the contract. There was a pound sign, followed by a number, followed by noughts. A lot of noughts. A fearsome number of noughts.

"Too much!" he yelped.

Lou fixed him with a bright green eye. "We know," she said.

"Hah!" said Morrie. He was getting his nerve back. "Plus I suppose you would like the Queen of England as hostess at the pre-gig cocktail reception?"

"There will, of course, be extras," said Lou. "But not with Her Maj in."

"You are not getting this, are you?" said Morrie. "It is normal in these circumstances for *you* to be the ones who give *me* a little present. By which I mean quite a big present. To persuade me. So I will let the band play. So they sell a lorra lorra records—Oi! Wozzat?"

90

"What's what?" said Lou.

"Whatever it is that is wrapped around my leg."

Lou peered under the table. "That's Georgina," she said, pushing her hair out of her face.

"Wha?"

"Georgina is a fer-de-lance," said Lou. "Such attractive coloring, do you not think? Plus, of course, the fer-de-lance is the deadliest snake in the world."

"Except the black mamba," said Buddy, frowning judiciously.

"The jury is out on that," said Lou, sticking up for her serpent.

"Be that as it may," said Enid, ever practical, "I know you are just longing to sign. Would you like to borrow a pen, or have you got one of your own?"

Morrie signed the contract with a shaking hand. "Now get that thing off me," he said.

"Georgina!" cried Lou sweetly. The serpent slithered good as gold into her mistress's Prada schoolbag and lay hissing contentedly. "Now, cheer up, Mr. Steam. Will it not be marvelous to have the legendary Death Eric on your stage just three short weeks from now?"

Morrie Steam grunted. The door closed. Sometimes he did not half wish he was still in scrap metal. He pulled a big box of money from his safe and began to count it. Some people swore by yoga or running marathons. Morrie Steam reckoned there was nothing as soothing as the feel of a big stash of fifty-pound notes ruffling through the fingers.

And, of course, the kid had been right. It would be great for Henge to have Death Eric's comeback performance.

A small, brilliant lightbulb appeared over Morrie Steam's head. He would put the ticket prices up a fiver each.

Now all he had to do was put Eric on the posters, lean back, and wait for the band to turn up.

Back in the Costa de Lott village hall, Death Eric had been getting well into it. Every day, bright and early at four thirty p.m. sharp, Eric, Fingers, and Kenyatta would be rubbing the sleep out of their eyes and thundering into the old faves. Every day at six, the FRYING TONITE signs would go up and in would troop the residents.

Thanks to Kenyatta, the residents were fatter nowadays. Quite a lot of them had taken to wearing black leather biker boots instead of Gucci loafers, and sleeveless denim jackets with skulls and chains instead of fur coats. Thanks to Fingers's lawn clinics, their lawns were a deep, brilliant green. Sid the Soothsayer had returned from his course with a small goatskin Spirit Drum and was doing his best to freak the rook colony before the rook colony freaked him. Eric was happy, as far as it was possible to tell. All in all, life was pretty good.

As for Enid and the children, they had things under control. Enid was busy organizing the Henge gig, though she had made sure nobody told the band about it in case they got nervous. Buddy had work to do, plus he wanted to practice his keyboards. Lou had fallen right behind with her reading and wanted to catch up.

Nobody had time to even think about Per.

And it did not occur to anyone that when life was this calm, a storm just had to be around the corner.

It would soon.

Anyway.

What with work and reading and one thing and another, ten days passed. On the eleventh, Enid said they had better go and break the Henge gig news to the band. So Buddy and Lou strolled over to the village hall.

The hall was vibrating like an enormous engine.

Chip fumes seeped from the open windows. Inside, the music was like a rogue bulldozer. Buddy stepped around a Cabinet minister trying to shake his head loose with headbanging. Lou made her way around the back of the vicar's wife, who was playing frenzied air guitar. They clambered on stage. Eric was playing the Doom Riff section of "Hop in the Cheese Vat, Irene," an infectious melody that had gone platinum on five continents. When his daughter's small, firm face appeared among the many scarves tied to his mike stand, he went white and his mouth fell open and his hands dropped off the guitar. Fingers and Kenyatta carried on for a bar or two, then trailed off with a sound like a thunderstorm leaving work and heading for home.

"Woooh!" said Eric, making the sign against the evil eye. "Haven't I seen you somewhere before?"

"I am your daughter," said Lou. "The opposite of your son."

"Oh," said Eric. "Yeah."

"And I am the son," said Buddy, appearing darkly on the other side of the mike stand.

The audience was shouting for more. Something huge sailed through the air and settled over the drum kit. It seemed to be the vicar's wife's knickers.

Buddy had wondered how to approach the Henge announcement. If he tried to break the news gently, his father might well become confused. Analysis pointed to a more direct approach. So he lifted up one side of green hair and shouted into the tattooed ear, "You've got a gig, Pa."

"Wha?" said Eric.

"Gig?" said Fingers and Kenyatta.

"Henge Festival," said Buddy.

"Ten days from now," said Lou.

Eric had shuffled to the back of the stage, where Sid the Soothsayer was fiddling with bones and pinches of colored stuff. "I dunno," he said.

"You have got the rooks under control," said Buddy.

"And if Fingers and Kenyatta don't play, they will be arrested," said Lou.

"Plus," said Buddy, "we have got you a seriously gigantic contract . . ."

"Contract?" said all three band members at once.

". . . that says you will be paid a fortune after you have played the gig, and not before."

There was a pause. Then the band said, all together, "Where was that?"

"Henge."

"Henge," they all said together, though the way it sounded, it might have been "Hinge," but, of course, the Henge Festival is world famous and there is no place called Hinge, or at least no place that sensible people have ever heard of. Though rock-and-roll artists are often the opposite of sensible, which is why they employ roadies. Roadies are the most sensible people in the world. Except Thick Rick, of course. Thick Rick chopped and stacked the firewood at Dunravin, and he usually put that in the wrong place.

"OK," said Buddy. "That's settled, then. The road crew will start getting things ready—"

"Stop!" cried Eric, raising a finger on whose final joint was tattooed the word STOP.

"Wha?" said Lou. She knew that when Eric took control, things went out of control.

"Sid was tellin' me some stuff he learned on his course," said Eric, jerking a thumb at Sid the Soothsayer, who had lit a small fire and started chanting. "We've gotta change everything. Right, Sid?"

Sid the Soothsayer grinned and fluttered his fingers. His anticurse course had indeed changed him. He had had every second tooth extracted, and

96

the ones that remained filed sharp and painted black. This made his grin rather alarming.

"For behold, it is apparently like written," said Eric, "that a simple van full of people shall go forth to Hinge—"

"Henge," said Buddy.

"—whatever, to get into the vibe, and they shall go in simplicity like unto a burger that saith, I need no bun, I shall let the, like . . . what, Sid?"

"The meat do the talking," said Sid.

"Like, the meat do the talking," said Eric. "And lo, the driver shall be Rick that is Thick, and no other."

Lou fixed her father with a stern green eye. "Enid does the driving," she said.

"Stop!" cried Eric, raising the tattooed finger again. "We must break the pattern! We shall go away, I and Fingers and Kenyatta plus Rick that is Thick, and, er . . ."

"Get it together?" said someone.

"Get it together, just the four of us—"

"Five."

"—whatever, alone," said Eric with astonishing clarity. "Get into the vibe, just us. I defy the raven! I have spoken." He turned to stalk out of the hall.

And there was Enid in a new floaty dress, leaning against the doorpost. "Catch him!" she cried.

Too late. Eric stalked into the wall on the wrong side of the door, said, "Sorry, man," and fell stunned to the ground.

"Thank goodness you're here," said Lou to Enid, as she dabbed her father's brow with witch hazel. "Dad wants to go to Henge without us, and he wants Thick Rick to drive. Apparently it will, like, break the curse. *Ridiculous!*"

An expression of doubt and unhappiness crossed Enid's face, like the shadow of a cloud passing over a huge but beautiful landscape. "Dunno," she said.

"*Wha?*"

"You gotta ask yourself, who pays the wages?" said Enid.

"*Enid!*" cried Lou.

"*What* wages?" cried Buddy.

Enid did her best to scowl. Normally, nightclub bouncers ran screaming from this scowl. But she loved the Thrashmettle kids, so she merely looked like a huge but beautiful landscape with indigestion.

"What is it?" said Lou, alarmed.

"Orders is orders," said Enid unhappily. "Gotta do what the Boss says. I'll talk to Thick Rick. I'll make sure that nothing that can go wrong will go wrong."

There was silence, broken only by the quiet crackle of Lou and Buddy's laser eyes.

"This is Dad we're talking about," said Buddy.

"Off on his own with just the band," said Lou.

"Guys!" said Sid, coming up behind them and grinning his ghastly grin. "It's going to be *fine!*"

Buddy let his gaze rest darkly on the soothsayer. Lou shook her head.

"Let us leave these people to their own devices, Enid," said Buddy. "If you need us, we will be at home, playing some music."

"In the Blue Room," said Lou.

The Blue Room was indeed an oasis of sense and calm. Lou picked up the violin, and Buddy sat at the keyboard, and they played *A Little Bit of Music* by Kling as the plaster ladies looked down from the ceiling.

As the final strains died away, Buddy said, "Nice one."

"One feels calmer now," said Lou.

"The band is playing OK. Sid seems to have made it OK with the rooks. Henge is a big, big festival, and they are on their way there to get into the vibe, which is OK. What's not to be calm about?"

Lou observed that, despite these encouraging words, her brother's face was shadowed, his dark eyes brooding. She said, "Things can . . . go wrong. We would be even calmer if Per were here."

"But he isn't," said Buddy, ever the realist. "And you are about to make a suggestion."

"I was thinking of ringing Trash Productions," said Lou, looking at him sideways.

"You mean the Trash Productions who did the Death Eric Worldwide Lookalike Competition?"

"Just in case," said Lou.

"Brilliant," said Buddy.

Loading the van for Henge caused a certain amount of trouble. First of all, Thick Rick got the wrong idea and filled it up with firewood. Then Fingers Trubshaw vanished, and was discovered three hours later in someone's backyard painting miracle fertilizer on a couple of yellow blades of grass he had noticed earlier. Then Kenyatta McClatter was found to be absent, and it was not until the wind changed that they were able to follow the burning-lard smoke trail to a gravel pit where Kenyatta was dishing out fish to an encampment of traveling folk. Then Eric himself seemed to have vanished off the face of the earth until Buddy chanced to hear a droning noise floating from one of the ventilators of the Rehearsal Bunker. Several roadies went down the endless steps and found him with Sid the Soothsayer in a pentacle chalked on the floor, burning disgusting candles and chanting.

But eventually Buddy and Lou stood under the mighty front porch of Dunravin as the Transit van, loaded with Death Eric, practice equipment, a mower, a fish fryer, and Sid the Soothsayer, started up. Thick Rick put a tattooed arm out of the driver's window and gave a Victory sign. "To Henge!" cried the voices from within. "In all simplicity!" Thick Rick put his foot on the gas. The Transit reversed sharply into an ornamental pond. Half a dozen roadies lifted it out, and someone showed Thick Rick how to put the van into first gear. "To Henge!" cried the voices in the van again. This time it roared off forward and was lost to view.

"I wonder if we'll ever see them again," said Lou.

"I told BB to put a homer on the van," said Enid.

"A homer?"

"They use them in James Bond films," said Buddy. "They sort of bleep, so you can find people if they get lost."

"Exactly," said Enid, pulling from her pocket a machine that looked like a miniature TV and pressing buttons with her giant thumbs. "Look."

On the screen was a map. In the middle of the map a light was flashing.

"Excellent," said Buddy and Lou. Then Buddy said, "It's not moving."

"Zoom in," said Lou.

Enid pressed more buttons. The picture became more detailed. "In that round thing. Near the house."

"That's this house," said Buddy.

"The round thing's a pond," said Lou.

"This pond," said Buddy. He rolled up his black sleeve, plunged his arm into the water, and came up with a little metal box. "Would this be a homer?" he said.

"Ye-es," said Enid.

"*The* homer?"

"Ye-es," said Enid.

There was silence. Then there was the beep of Lou's telephone as she dialed. "Hello?" she said.

"Trash Productions? Gimme the boss. This is an emergency."

News of the Henge booking had got around fast. It was all over the music papers and all over the Net. On their way to buy sheet music for Schlump's *Medium Sized Music for Calm Coffee Break*, Buddy and Lou were doorstepped by eighty photographers. DEATH ERIC COMEBACK? yelled the tabloid papers. DEFINITELY! yelled the new posters Morrie Steam had had printed.

Things were not actually as definite as Morrie Steam would have liked everyone to think. On the morning of the fourth day before the gig, Enid issued the final orders. "Roadies, get the trucks together. We'll be hauling out day after tomorrow."

"Check," said the roadies as one roadie.

All that day and the day after, there was the sound of forklifts rumbling and articulated lorry trailers clashing in the huge industrial complex that held Death Eric's equipment. The only thing that did not arrive was Death Eric.

But, of course (said Buddy to Lou, sounding slightly hoarse), they were already at or somewhere near Henge, getting into the vibe.

Of course they were (said Lou to Buddy, her voice croaking a little).

Then they went back to making phone calls. They had been making a lot of phone calls.

It was actually a bit worrying. No one had seen Death Eric.

Maybe they would just turn up. Enid said they usually had, in the past.

But this was the present.

Actually, it was more than a bit worrying.

It was very worrying indeed.

The Spearmint Vanguard were doing mostly school assembly gigs nowadays. This Thursday, they were playing their usual weary blend of folk music and easy listening in the hall at Tortoise Lofts Junior School. They had jogged offstage to the polite but unenthusiastic clapping of the children, several of whom had gone to sleep during "Froggy Went a-Wooing," the storming finale of the set. They had walked into their dressing room, which was actually the boys' changing room.

Waiting under a row of coat pegs were a smart looking girl in a wine-red school blazer and a dark boy dressed in black. Derek Protheroe, the

Spearmints' leader, was about to sign autographs for them when he saw their eyes. The girl's were green and piercing. The boy's were dark and hot. Both sets were strangely hypnotic, as if their owners were on a mission and would not be denied. His head swam. He stayed upright only because a huge, beautiful woman with tattooed knees and a print dress stepped out of the shower cubicle, locked the changing-room door, and hung him on a coat peg.

"Who are you?" said Derek to the children, in a rather strangled voice.

"That is not important," said the girl, who, close up, looked small, immaculate, and tough as rawhide. "We got your name from Trash Productions. You are a Death Eric tribute band, right?"

"Nah," said Derek, with as glittering a smile as he could manage in the difficult circumstances. "I mean, we were once. Breath Derek, we were called. But we changed our policy when we started playing schools. Went for something a little smoother."

"We want you to do a gig," said Lou. "As Death Eric."

"Nah," said Derek, with his smile. "My conscience would not permit it."

"We are artists," said the Spearmint Vanguard's bassist, who looked like a tame version of Fingers Trubshaw, though it was hard to be sure with him hiding behind a locker like that.

"Committed to our music," said the drummer, who looked like a watered-down edition of Kenyatta McClatter, though it was difficult to be certain with him having locked himself in one of the lavs like that.

"You do not understand," said the boy, who looked slim, immaculate, and dangerously intelligent. "Enid will explain."

"We need you to play one gig," said Enid. "We will pay you big money. This is not an offer you can walk away from—"

"Just you watch," said Derek bravely from his peg. "Tribute bands are so . . . *village hall*. Plus, I hate the taste of bat and snakes give me the creeps."

"—because," said Enid, "many people find it hard to walk with broken legs."

Derek's face suddenly matched his teeth, which were snow white. "Come to think of it," he said, "I have been thinking for a while now that it would be great to play the old tunes again."

"Me too," said the bassist from behind the lockers.

"And me," said the drummer from inside the lav.

"Who said anything about playing?" said Buddy.

The Spearmint Vanguard laughed with great heartiness at they knew not what. Buddy and Lou felt a deep, warm relief. They hated violence.

"See you at Henge, then, day after tomorrow," said Enid. "Be there or be in intensive care."

"Lovely," cried Morrie Steam, running his meaty hands through a big bucket of banknotes. "Everyone wants tickets. Wadsa wonga." His chilly eyes swiveled onto Lou, in the corner reading a book, and Buddy, who was sitting by his sister, reading the Junior Investor pages of the *Financial Times*. "Now, kids. What was that you said about a new rider?"

"We want a totally private dressing room," said Lou, looking up from her book.

"We want to control the stage lights," said Buddy, folding his newspaper. "Like, total control."

"And we want no strangers near the mixing board," said Lou.

"The settings are unique and confidential," said Buddy, frowning. "Plus, there is a lot of espionage about."

"Masses," said Lou, smiling sweetly.

"And if I say naff off?" said Morrie threateningly.

"Bit of hush in the Eric department," said Lou with a charming smile.

"Dead silence, actually," said Buddy, gazing moodily out of the window.

For a day and a half he had been combing the approach roads to Henge for a white van with Thick Rick at the helm. He and Lou had made hundreds of phone calls, sent encyclopedias of text messages, and alerted the police of five counties. It was just dead nerve-racking, was what it was. The person who really knew how to deal with it was—

"Your dad's manager," said Morrie. "Per, innit? What's happened to him?"

"Having a bit of a break," said Lou, going a little pink.

"Rang up this morning," said Morrie.

"He did?" said the children, keenly excited. "Where did he ring from?"

"Didn't say," said Morrie. "Bought a racehorse off me. Wasn't cheap, neither. Quite a stable he's got nowadays."

"He has?" said the children.

"Spendin' money like a drunken sailor," said Morrie. "Bless his heart. It is the duty of the rock 'n' roll band leader to make the fortune of the race horse breeder."

"Per's a really clever guy," said Lou, with genuine admiration.

"Brilliant," said Buddy, with total sincerity.

"Yes. Well, you'll want to be gettin' your dad ready." Morrie plunged his hands to the elbows in a soothing vat of money.

Flashing their laminates, the children went into the backstage yard. The Death Eric artics were backed up against the stage, and the crew were rolling out industrial-sized amplifiers and lighting rigs.

But of the white Tranny, there was no sign.

Two hundred miles away, in a skittle alley behind a pub called the Fox and Wreckage, Death Eric were having a band meeting. The gear was set up at the end of the skittle alley. All 110 inhabitants of the village were in the public bar.

"So where," said Trubshaw, "is the festival?"

"Maybe's a low turnout this year," said Eric.

"Fish, anyone?" said Kenyatta McClatter.

"Tell me," said Eric, "what's cider made of?"

"Dunno. D'you want a bit more?"

"Bit more what?" said Eric, rising to turn on the TV.

The screen showed a huge green bowl of land with a stage in the middle. Music came from the speakers: metal music, familiar as an old pair of shoes.

"Someone's playing 'Pig Train'!" said Fingers.

The camera zoomed in. It focused on a black drummer in a tam-o'-shanter, a bassist with curly brown hair and a three-piece tweed suit, and a man with curtains of green hair, round red spectacles, and a gnawed black Gibson Flying V.

"That's us!" said Kenyatta.

The singer bit into a bat. He kicked the mike stand covered in scarves across the stage.

"Nah," said Eric. "Wrong tattoos."

"That's a relief," said Fingers.

"Uncanny, for a minute there," said Kenyatta.

There was silence.

"I bin thinking," said Eric.

"You *wha*?" said his sidemen, astonished.

"About what cider's made of."

"Wha?"

But Eric was at the pay phone, stabbing buttons.

*

Behind the mixing board at Henge, Buddy and Lou sat still as statues as the last howling note of Rabid Dingo faded into the hills.

"Take the gear down," said Enid into her portable radio.

She leaned forward and popped the CD to which Breath Derek had been miming out of its slot in the mixing board. On the stage, the little figures of the tribute band pranced and bowed and looked incredibly pleased with themselves, except for the one with the black guitar, who was spitting out bat fur.

"They want to do an encore," said the voice from the set.

"Mention the word 'legs,'" said Enid.

There was a brief silence. The little figures stopped prancing and scuttled off the stage, looking nervously over their shoulders.

Then the voice said, "They want to go home."

"And go home they shall," said Enid. "And so shall we, once we pick up the wonga. I'll just nip round and do it."

She was gone ten minutes. When she came back, she looked pale and, for Enid, faint.

"What is it?" said Lou.

"Morrie Steam. He sent a check. To Per."

"Is that good?" said Buddy and Lou.

"Maybe yes, maybe no," said Enid, looking gloomy. "On the bad side, we don't know where he is, we've got no money, any minute now the house will be full of bailiffs again, we've lost your dad, and Per's buying sports cars and racehorses. On the good side, er, dunno. It would be a good thing if you could make your own instruments and wear your old clothes."

"Out of the question," said the two children as one kid.

"So?"

"We shall find Dad. And next time, we shall get paid in cash."

"Hmph," said Enid. "Last time your dad went off like this was after the raven gig. He didn't come back for a year."

"That was when we were little," said Lou.

"We are bigger now," said Buddy grimly. His telephone rang. "Yeah?" he said. Then, "Dad?"

There was sudden silence, broken only by the wild cheering of half a million festival-goers. "Where are you?" said Buddy.

"Stupid question," said Enid. "Obviously, he won't know."

A pause. "Public phone?" said Buddy. "Cider? It's made out of apples, mostly, if you're lucky. Dad, where are you?" He held the receiver away from him. "He's hung up."

"Give me that," said Lou. She grabbed the phone and punched buttons. "Right," she said. "Ring-back." Then, "It's engaged."

"When did he ever put a phone back on the hook?" said Buddy.

Lou considered. "My sixth birthday party. After he had ordered the pizza."

"Yeah. Then. Wrong phone on the wrong hook," said Buddy, clutching his spiky black hair.

"Whoa there, hoss," said Lou, unbuttoning the special pocket in which she kept the *Tales from the Brothers Grime*. "Don't worry, we'll find him."

As Lou leafed through the improving volume, Buddy paced up and down, scowling. He did not hold with fairy stories. He decided to work out his father's whereabouts by more reliable means, i.e., pure logic. His chain of reasoning went like this.

1) Public telephones were weird and old school. So wherever Eric was holed up, it was probably somewhere quite hilly and therefore without a mobile phone signal.

2) It was probably somewhere in England or

America, because that is where people drink cider. And American cider is only apple juice and Eric was not the kind of person who liked apple juice, so the evidence pointed to England.

3) Wherever he was, he would have got there because of a stupid mistake.

4) Wherever he was, it must be quite nice, otherwise he would not have stayed there, unless, of course, it was somewhere quite difficult to find the way out of.

All in all, the evidence pointed to a pub in a cider orchard in a picturesque ravine or coal mine at the end of a one-way street.

"So all we have to do is to identify such places and search them thoroughly," he said.

"Ye-es," said Lou, frowning. "But how to find them?"

Buddy shrugged. "Not my problem," he said.

"Quite," said Lou. "Well, this is all very helpful. And if I add to it some ideas from 'Nigel and the Jewel Beyond Price—'"

"Wha?" said Enid.

Lou opened her well-thumbed *Brothers Grime*. "'Once upon a time—'"

"Condense," said Buddy. "Shorten. Précis."

"'A bad wizard stole a jewel off this guy Nigel,'" said Lou, very happy, for she loved to read aloud. "'So Nigel went to a good wizard and asked him how to get the jewel back. And the good wizard said, "Go to the Castle of the Moon and find the Cap of Invisibility. Then go to the Crags of the Wind and find the Brogues of Flying. Wearing these, flit to the bad wizard's castle. There, you will find two doors. One is guarded by a huge man with a sword who always tells the truth. The other is guarded by a huge man with a sword who always tells lies. Devise the question that will get you into the right door, and beware, for if you ask wrong, you will be sliced into tiny—"'

"' "Thank you very much," said Nigel, reversing out of the room.'

"' "Oi!" cried the wizard. "I haven't finished!"'

"'But Nigel was already in the road.'

"'He walked until he found a police station. "Excuse me," he said to the officer on duty. "But this bad wizard has nicked my jewel."'

"'So the policeman knocked on the front door of the castle, arrested the swordsmen for threatening behavior, and told the wizard to give Nigel his jewel back.' Which [it says here] goes to show," said Lou, "that there is a short way round and a long way round."

"But—" said Buddy.

"One moment," said Lou. She dialed Directory Assistance and found the area code Eric had called from. "There," she said.

The area covered about 400 square miles of the Old Stone Hills. So into the Old Stone Hills purred the Caddy, knocking cyclists into banks of cow parsley, sideswiping dry stone walls, leaving tire marks on village greens, and generally having a great day out in the country. They slept that night in a pleasant inn, at which the roadies earned the goodwill of all by building an extension and Buddy and Lou made a small fortune on the quiz machine, Buddy doing the math questions and Lou the arty ones. And bright and early the next afternoon, the Caddy purred between mown green verges into the outskirts of a village of little gray houses set between lawns as green as Lou's eyes. A sign slid toward the Caddy's windscreen. Lou read it aloud for the benefit of the roadies, who tended to have a bit of trouble with the printed word even when the letters were six inches high.

"Welcome to—"

"I'll kill him," hissed Enid, tromping hard on the Caddy's gas pedal and slapping two extra nicotine patches on her leg.

"—Hinge."

"This int Henge," said a roadie.

"No," said Enid. "It is Hinge."

"So what are we doing here?"

"That," said Enid, "is a question you had better ask Thick Rick when we see him."

"There he is," said the roadie. "Over there. Standing, like."

"Oooh yes," said Enid, stomping on the brake and rolling up her floral sleeves to reveal vast forearms.

"Oops," said the roadie. "Seems to have gone."

For Thick Rick, demonstrating a surprising flash of intelligence, was indeed pegging it for the horizon as fast as his knobbly legs would carry him.

Over the noise of birds singing and the tick of the cooling Caddy and the crash of tackety boots as Thick Rick hurdled a chicken coop came a new sound: the roar of an electric guitar.

"Dad!" cried Buddy and Lou.

"Hist!" said Enid, raising a scarlet-nailed forefinger for silence.

They listened. It was like "Pig Train," but not "Pig Train"; like "Chainsaw," but not "Chainsaw." Looking around, Lou saw heads—hard, thick roadie heads—start to twitch. Twitching became nodding. Nodding became banging.

"New material," breathed Buddy.

"*Great* new material," breathed Lou.

"Oh, I dunno," said Sid the Soothsayer, sticking his head in the Caddy window. "Usual old rubbish. Nobody'll buy it, I reckon—oi!"

For Enid had enfolded him in a bone-crushing grasp and was covering his spotty face with kisses.

They followed the music to the Fox and Wreckage. The bar was empty, except for a jolly red barman pulling pints of cider and plunking them on trays.

"Where is everybody?" said Enid, though, of course, the words were inaudible.

"Little valley," said Lou, lip-reading.

"Skittle alley," said Buddy, lip-writing and piling through the door at the back of the bar.

The skittle alley was jammed with rustics, pogoing and headbanging. A stout ploughman crowd-surfed from the dartboard to the GENTS sign and vanished through the door with a bubbling cry.

"Cooking," said Lou to her brother.

"Hot," said Buddy to his sister.

Neither of them could lip-read accurately, and a nasty argument might have started, but just in the nick of time, the song ended.

"Hangyou hangyou," boomed their father's voice in the silence. "That was a new tune called 'Where's the Festival?'" He paused to eat deeply from a bag of bat scratchings. "An frour nex number, we'd like to do, er"—Fingers Trubshaw was seen to whisper passionately in his ear—"Wha, Fingers, what was that again?"

More whispering.

"'Nother new song, 'You're Stone Deaf, You Twit.' No, sorry, 'We Are Really Really Lost.' A-one, two, three, er . . ."

And away they went.

It was blinding. It was shattering. Buddy and Lou watched their father in a warm, bright haze.

A haze as bright as new scientific instruments. As warm as cashmere blazers.

They had found Death Eric.

And Death Eric had found the groove.

They held a meeting in the Caddy.

"So," said Buddy, "what now?"

"Well," said Enid, "the boys are playing lovely."

"Check."

"So we"ll get Running Dave down from Hoot Zoot Records. The A&R man."

"A&R?" said Lou—largely, dear reader, for your benefit.

"Artists and Repertoire, it stands for. Meaning, he is the geezer what decides whether your dad's got enough new stuff to make a new record."

"Running Dave?" said Buddy.

"Full-blooded member of the Cree Nation by adoption."

"Ah. Well, call him now. And then?"

"Make a new record. Fix up a proper tour to promote it. Make sure we keep our eye on the band."

"If this Running Dave likes the music," said Buddy.

"How could he not?" said Enid.

"It is certainly very good," said Lou. "Even we think so."

"What I mean," said Enid, "is that this Running Dave probably uses his feet a lot, and he is not going to get around so well if I stand on them a bit."

"Ah," said Buddy.

"I dunno," said Sid the Soothsayer, frowning. "I got a bad feeling—oi!" For Enid had thrown herself upon him and was covering his face with rough kisses.

"Order," said Lou, tapping the table with an ebony gavel. "So we make the records, fix the tour, and get a lot of money."

"Sort of," said Enid.

Four painfully bright eyes, two brown, two green, swiveled onto the gigantic roadie.

"The thing is," said Enid, blushing, "that money doesn't come to us."

"Don't tell me," said Buddy.

"It goes to Per," said Lou.

"To the Management office," said Enid.

"But you've already been there," said Buddy.

"Not actually," said Enid.

"Why *not?*"

"*Honestly!*" said Lou. "Don't you understand *anything?*" She took Enid's mighty hand. "Some people know nothing," she said.

Enid shook her head. "Buddy's right," she said. "I should have gone. But I didn't like to, in case I found him and asked him questions he didn't like and that made him hate me."

"But you're fearless!" cried Buddy.

"So are you," said Lou. "But imagine someone asking you to write a new story about what you did on your holidays. There are some things even fearless people can't do."

"So when Running Dave has been," said Enid, sticking out her huge, beautiful jaw, "I will go to Smoke City and visit the Management office and find Per and ask him what the exact heck is going down." She said it in a firm voice. But she did not feel all that firm. What if she saw Per and the old magic was still there? Then she would have to choose between him and the kids . . .

Peeling the backing off a nicotine patch, she slapped it onto her leg. She would cross that bridge when she came to it. Meanwhile, there was work to do.

"It'll be fine," said Sid the Soothsayer. "It'll all—"

"SHURRUP!" cried everyone in the Caddy.

Enid called the record company. Running Dave said he was on his way.

At eight o'clock that evening, the sun was sinking

toward the round green hills on the horizon, and the Thrashmettle kids were eating a dinner of homemade pies and beans on a picnic table on the village green.

Buddy stopped eating and cocked an ear. "What's that?" he said.

Lou cocked another. "Thunder?" she said.

"Too regular."

"Heartbeat?"

"Too loud."

Buddy noticed that the surface of the milk in his glass was now broken into little ripples by a strange, rhythmic booming noise. All around their feet, earthworms were heaving themselves out of the ground to escape whatever it was that was making their burrows shudder. There was a long, heartrending screech of tires. And around the corner on two wheels drifted the most sophisticated van Buddy had ever seen.

It was a snow-white lowrider with coal-black windows. Its roof sprouted aerials of many designs. The sound of its exhaust pipe was as the mutter of a multitude. The boom of its bass bins was so mighty that the van itself kept vibrating in and out of focus.

Lou and Buddy did not impress easily, but they

were impressed now. The van driver heaved on the handbrake. The van did a 180°. The engine shut off and so did the stereo. For a second it sat quiet and blind in its personal dust cloud. Then the driver's door opened and a man got down.

"Running Dave," said Enid out of the side of her mouth.

He was dressed in black from head to foot, with a discreet silver and turquoise bootlace tie. He opened the passenger door and the prettiest cowgirl Lou had ever seen fed her legs into the world.

"Loopabella van Squee," breathed Enid admiringly.

Loopabella van Squee had white doeskin fringes, a short little skirt, and white lizardskin cowboy boots. She batted her rhinestone eyelashes and said, "Why, honey, you're so *cute!*"

"Likewise," said Lou, secure in the classic elegance of her school uniform.

"Nice suit, man," said Running Dave to Buddy.

"Likewise," said Buddy, though he had reservations about the bootlace tie.

"Where's the band?" said Running Dave.

A crowd of roadies ushered the two Very Important People into the skittle alley. A table had been stationed in front of the stage. It was draped in the skull and crossbones. On it were a plate of bat scratchings, various bottles, a notepad, and some freshly sharpened pencils.

"Pray be seated," said Enid, drawing out a chair with a flourish. "Tequila?"

"Thank you, no," said the Very Important People, pouring each other glasses of mineral water.

Running Dave snapped fingers crusted with silver rings. "Commence!" he cried.

The curtain rose. There were several explosions and a cloud of green smoke. The deck started playing rustic heyho music loud enough to blow panes out of the windows. Death Eric came on stage, heads bowed, fists raised in salute, and strapped on guitars. Behind the heyho music, a guitar started feeding back. The feedback came to the front of the mix. Roadies with willow branches fanned away the smoke. The first mighty chords of "Where's the Festival?" thundered into the room.

The door behind Running Dave's table was full of heads. At first they had a purplish look, as if everyone was holding their breath. Then Eric and the boys got in the groove, and much breath left many lungs in a large collective whoosh. Then, one by one, the heads started to smile.

For Running Dave was nodding and Loopabella's cowgirl hat was twitching. The nod became deeper, the twitch more pronounced. Forty bars in, Running Dave was headbanging like a woodpecker.

From then on, it all went swimmingly. People started giving each other high fives. Villagers burst in from the bar. There was uncontrolled dancing. After "We Are Really Really Lost," the band mingled with the record company folk. It was a happy occasion, with a merry buzz of conversation. Kenyatta McClatter fried a spot of catfish for Loopabella, and Fingers Trubshaw got down to a serious garden-maintenance conversation with Running Dave, who was worried about the lawn on his Docklands roof. Eric had wandered off somewhere, as usual. Someone started singing folk songs—

When suddenly, from outside the hall, there came a long, frightful wail.

The kids rushed out.

Eric was standing in front of Running Dave's van. His right hand was clapped to his forehead. His left hand was pointing wordlessly at the van's bonnet. "Wooo," he was saying. "Heav*eee*. Wooo."

"What is it, Dad?" said Lou, her face all white and worried.

"Dad?" said Buddy, his face the same color as his sister's.

Eric turned to them, wild-eyed behind the red glasses. "The bird," he said.

"Bird?"

"*Gkkk*," said Eric, pointing.

What he was pointing at was the hood ornament. The hood ornament that was in the shape of a dark enameled bird, with eyes made from what were probably genuine rubies.

"What *are* you on about?" said Lou.

"It's not a raven," said Buddy.

"Ravens are birds," said Eric.

"All ravens are birds," said Buddy. "But not all birds are ravens."

"Wha?"

"That," said Lou, "is a bald eagle, totem bird of the Native American peoples."

"Looks like a raven to me," said Eric. His face had vanished behind the green curtains of hair. His head was shaking.

"Be that as it may," said Enid brightly, "Running Dave likes the songs. So we're off into the studio. Great, eh?"

But Eric's hair was moving from side to side like

seaweed on a rock. "Nevermore," he was muttering. "The curse returns. Where's Sid? Bop a Spirit Drum, someone."

"Never mind Sid," said Enid, her warm smile tinged with agony. "You're off to Castle Bones. The future lies ahead, and it is bright, bright, bright!"

"Certainly looks that way," said Sid the Soothsayer, coming out of the skittle alley.

"ShadDAP!" cried everybody.

Half an hour later, the limos pulled out of Hinge and headed east. Enid waved them off, then headed for the Musicians' Quarter of Smoke City and her date with Destiny.

Enid approached the Musicians' Quarter slowly. There was no sense rushing to see Per. She had decided to be calm and subtle.

So on arrival in Smoke City, she had her hair done in cornrows and tied at the back with a beaded ribbon. Then she bought a new supply of nicotine patches and slapped on two. Then she bought a new pair of shoes, large, red, with high heels; a shady hat; and a handbag, in which she put a notebook full of things she wanted Per to explain. As she walked through the palm trees and Cadillacs outside the

Tower of Power, where the world's heaviest music managers had their offices, she knew she was looking her best.

The revolving doors whirred like a cooling fan in her wake. In the lift, she stabbed the PENTHOUSE button. The lift started to rise the fifty-five floors to the penthouse.

The butterflies in Enid's stomach were telling her what would happen next.

The lift would stop. The doors would open. She would step into a lobby upholstered in black rubber with a desk made out of a ragged steel sheet. Behind the desk would be sitting a nice blond girl wearing very small black leather clothes and ripped fishnet tights. The sign over the girl's head would say DOOM MANAGEMENT.

The lift stopped. The doors opened. Enid slapped an extra nicotine patch on her leg and stepped into the familiar lobby.

Hang on a minute.

The lobby was upholstered in pink velvet with a desk made of brown wood and curly gold bits. Behind the desk sat a girl with black hair in a beehive and a baggy gingham check dress that came down to her ankles. The sign over the girl's head said HONEY BLINKS MANAGEMENT—HAVE A NICE DAY.

"Wrong floor," said Enid.

"It's always the right floor for Honey Blinks, the Midwest's Sweetheart," said the dark girl, smiling like a robot and talking like a machine. "Line dancers stand in *line* for Honey—"

"I was looking for Doom Management," said Enid. "In the penthouse."

"Why, this *is* the penthouse," said the gingham beehive robot. "Home of Honey—Hey! Where are you goin'?"

Too late. Enid and her power shoes had marched through the door behind the desk. "Who runs this place?" she said.

"Me," said a small, nervous man who had come out of an office down the corridor.

"Who did you rent it from?"

"Power Office Rentals," said the man. "About my door—"

"Oops," said Enid, looking down and noticing that the door was indeed still in her hand. "Have it back." She threw it to him, spun on her heel, and walked away.

Behind her, the small man's shoes stuck out from

under the door. They twitched faintly. Enid paid no attention. As far as she was concerned, Per was a rat, and a rat on the run. In the process he had scorned her. Hell had no fury like an Enid scorned. Now she was going to visit Power Office Rentals and find out if they knew where Per was. And she was going to track him down.

Granite-jawed and burning with loyalty and lost love, Enid stepped into the lift and started stabbing buttons. They broke. Leaving the lift, she got into another one. This time, she stabbed less powerfully. The doors closed. She was on the trail.

Castle Bones lay in the valley of the River Dusk. The suburbs of Smoke City had crept out toward it, but their neat rows of houses had never actually come within sight of it, the way Sunday picnickers tend to leave quite a bit of space around the local rattlesnake. For Castle Bones was the world's leading feedback metal recording studio and was generally thought to be the abode of Dark Forces. It was Death Eric's absolute favorite, and they had recorded several great albums there. It was all towers and pointed arches and gargoyles and Early Analog recording technology. It was set in huge gardens from whose grottoes and ravines the darkness seemed somehow never to clear. It was a weird, poisonous place, and normal families would not go anywhere near it in case they got bats in their hair. Naturally, Death Eric and the little Thrashmettles absolutely loved it.

But tonight, as the limos rolled through the crags and forests of yew trees that protected Castle Bones from the world, the band's mood was somber. Buddy pointed out a vampire bat wheeling in an updraft. Eric merely grunted. Lou drew his attention to a night-black snake gnawing something that squeaked on a branch over the drive. Eric said, "Yeah, dear." It was impossible to avoid the idea that he was brooding. And when they were greeted by beautiful Gothalinda, the manageress, in the black-carpeted Hall of Columns, Eric merely nodded and grunted and trailed off to bed. Which was weird, because it was only eleven o'clock at night, an hour when he would normally have been having breakfast.

During the next few days, life at Castle Bones settled into its steady rock-and-roll rhythm. Kenyatta McClatter moved into the kitchens and started frying everything in sight. Fingers Trubshaw chatted with the gardeners about plants that thrived in darkness. Everyone rode motorbikes, played darts with throwing knives, watched horror films, and lassoed longhorn cattle.

Everyone, that is, except Eric.

Eric sat in the Hall of Columns and stared into the pond as if he expected to see the future there, instead of green slime and toads. Whenever someone said something to him, he said, "Nevermore," and shook his head.

Even Gothalinda was worried about him. One night at dusk, when she had come all pale and cool from the cellar where she slept, she took the children aside and gave them glasses of strong Ribena. "Dollinks," she said, putting her black-nailed hands on theirs, "your poor papa."

"He feels he is under a curse," said Lou.

"Who isn't?" said Gothalinda, sighing. "I left a chainsaw in his bedroom. I vas thinkink it vould brink back the old days. I vas wronk. Not vun stick of furniture has he destroyed. He is so depressed, far, far away. But you can save him, I am sure. You are so younk, so wital, so full of blood . . . I mean, life."

"Would you mind not licking your lips like that?"

said Buddy, sidling between the manageress and his sister.

"Sorry," said Gothalinda, with her sweet, sharp smile. "But the days are tickink avay. The band must be in the studio tomorrow, I think. Because soon vill be full moon. And you know, Igor the engineer, the full moon . . ."

The children did not know. But given the amount of hair on Igor's face, they did not want to find out, either.

"We will do our beast. I mean best," said Buddy.

"Can't say fairer zan zat," said Gothalinda, and she got up. "Vell, don't forget ze garlic. Oh, I am a sucker for childrenz. Schleep sound, lieblings." She glided away.

Later that night, the children were woken by the sound of tires outside. Buddy scrambled out of his carved four-poster and went onto the balcony. A huge figure in a print dress was crunching in the half moonlight across the white animal skulls of the car park. "Enid!" he hissed.

The face looked up, huge and pale in the moonglow.

"Come up," he said.

A minute later, she was in the room.

"Nice *shoes*," said Lou.

"Thanks," said Enid, pulling them off and throwing them into the wastepaper basket.

"Any luck?" said Buddy.

"No," said Enid.

"Are you all right?" said Lou.

"Fine," said Enid, slapping another nicotine patch on her leg.

"So what does all this mean?" said Buddy.

"Means it's bedtime. Talk in the morning. Recording tomorrow. Goodnight."

"Goodnight."

Enid went.

"She doesn't seem too happy," said Lou.

"You think? Well, I'm glad she's back."

"Me too," said Lou. Castle Bones was fun, but it was the kind of place where it was nice to be sure that you had at least one sensible friend who ate normal food.

Buddy and Lou went back to sleep. Oddly, it was a happy sleep. For at bottom they were normal children and they were looking forward to the special excitement of a Death Eric recording morning.

*

At eleven sharp, a hunchbacked minion brought them breakfast in bed, and they washed, dressed, and went about their tasks.

Ever since they had been tiny, it had been Buddy and Lou's task to wake the members of Death Eric on recording days. It had become a sort of ritual. So it was with a sense of keen anticipation that they pulled the crash cart out of the room service cupboard and wheeled it along the corridor.

First on the list was Fingers Trubshaw, a dim, smelly shape under the covers. Buddy wheeled the cart up to the bedside and flicked a switch. A red light came on.

"Armed," he said.

"Fire one," said Lou.

Buddy pressed the button.

Three inches from Fingers's ear, an L.A.-model police siren started up full blast. Fingers shot out of bed and landed on his feet. "Wha?" he said.

"The police wish to interview you in connection with dead lawns and burning houses," said Lou.

"*Aieee!* " cried Fingers, leaping for the window.

"It's only us," said Lou, laughing heartily as they dragged him back to safety.

"Perishers."

"And if you go back to bed, we'll do it again," said Buddy.

Trubshaw nodded gloomily. He knew this to be true.

In Kenyatta's room, the children used the fire siren, with roughly the same results. They had turbo water jets ready for their father. As usual, he was not in the bed. Instead he was sleeping peacefully in the wardrobe, guarded by a couple of bats.

"Don't let off the water jets, poor Dad," said Lou.

"I wasn't going to," said Buddy.

"Athelstan!" muttered Eric in his sleep. "Tritium!"

"What's he on about?" said Lou.

"Ancient British kings," said Buddy. "Atom bomb ingredients. Who knows what goes on in that mighty brain? Dad! Wakey-wakey!"

Eric opened his eyes, one brown, one green. When he saw his kids he gave them a great white smile. "'Ello, smalls," he said. "I was having a dream about raincoats."

"Raining, was it?"

"Just raincoats."

The children pulled him affectionately to his feet

and showed him the difference between the room window and the bathroom door, in case of accidents.

Downstairs, Enid was sitting at the kitchen table, drinking tea and looking tired.

"So what about Per?" said Buddy.

"He's scarpered," said Enid.

"He'll have his reasons," said Lou confidently.

"Brilliant man like him," said Buddy.

Enid put her cup down in her saucer with something of a crash. "During the past week," she said, "I have followed Mr. Spire's trail down front alleys, back alleys, and blind alleys. I have visited his companies and the companies that belong to his companies. I have hung out in his favorite bars and supermarkets. I have intercepted mail, tapped phones, and set honey traps—"

"Honey traps?" said Buddy.

"Putting people into sticky situations," said Lou.

"—without result. The reason Per Spire has scarpered is that he wished to be gone and he does not wish us to find him. He has done what lawyers call a runner, and he has taken our money with him."

Buddy and Lou stared at her in stunned silence. Then Lou said, "I am *so* sorry."

"What for?" said Enid, blushing fiercely. "Anyway, mum's the word, or we'll upset the band. We'll deal with this. Any questions?"

"Would you like to borrow my hankie?" said Lou.

"Absolutely."

There was silence, broken by nose blowing. Then Buddy said, "Who needs Per anyway? We've got Enid. We've got you. And we've got me."

"Books!" cried Lou.

"Scientific instruments!" cried Buddy.

"Revenge!" cried Enid.

Lou's green eyes were shining brilliantly through happy tears. "Buddy!" she cried.

"Lou!" cried her brother.

"Enid!" they both cried.

"Lou! Buddy!" cried Enid.

It was a sickening display, but they all knew what it meant. What it meant was that Death Eric rocked and ruled.

And that sooner or later, Per Spire was toast.

That afternoon the band came down, ate a hearty breakfast, and filed into the studio, where Igor was gibbering in the control booth. The gear was all set up.

"'Vere's the Festival?'" said Igor.

"I dunno," said Eric, who was looking nervously around him for ravens of evil intent.

"Sonk title, silly," said Igor with a toothy simper. "Tape rollink. Ready ven you are. 'Vere's the Festival?' Take Vun."

If you put all the time Death Eric had spent in recording studios end to end, it would have added up to about twelve years. So they should have been completely professional, ready to blast into the number, knock it on the head, and drop it in the can. Buddy and Lou sat behind the stained-glass window that separated the artists from the control room, ready to bang heads. But as the great chords sounded, their heads failed to bang. Their hearts sank instead.

Death Eric was playing rubbish.

Igor was frowning too, as far as it was possible to detect facial expressions behind the thick mat of dark hair. "Vere is producer?" he said.

"No producer," said Buddy.

"Vere is normal producink guy?"

The normal producing guy was Per.

"We don't know," said Buddy.

"Or care," said Lou.

"Vell," said Igor, moving sliders with his curiously taloned hands. "Ve're goink to need somethink." He glanced at a Year Planner behind the mixing desk. The weeks of full moon were blocked off. In red. The next one was in three days. "Soon," he said.

"Keep trying," said Buddy.

So Igor kept trying. He tried recording live. He tried recording Eric as a guide track, then Kenyatta and Fingers together and separately, then Eric doing the big guitar riffs. At ten o'clock that night, everyone sat and listened to the playback. When it ended, there was a grim silence.

"Well?" said Enid.

"Tosh," said Fingers.

"Rubbish," said Kenyatta.

"Dates taste really nice," said Eric.

"How about the music?"

"Music?"

There was a general clutching of brows.

"The not-very-good music."

Eric nodded, dimly recalling a large, disorganized noise. "Per'll fix it," he said.

"Per's not here."

"He'll be back," said Eric.

Enid shot Buddy a glance. Lou raised her eyes from the book she had been reading. Not surprisingly, it was *Tales from the Brothers Grime.* She said, "Why don't we all sleep on it?"

"Sleep?" said Kenyatta.

"On it?" said Trubshaw.

"It's rubbish," they both said together with the perfect timing only a rhythm section that has played together for years can achieve. "Record companies don't pay for rubbish."

"Now, now," said Lou, snapping shut the *Tales.* "It will all look different in the morning. Chop-chop!"

And all the control room found themselves on their feet, heading for their bedrooms. All, that is, except Igor, who was heading for his staff accommodation in the stables; and Lou, who held Buddy by the sleeve.

"It's OK," called Lou to Enid. "We'll turn off the lights when we come to bed."

The soundproof door wheezed shut.

"OK," said Buddy. "What's the plan?"

"It's in the *Brothers Grime,*" said Lou. "Now please be quiet as a mouse, for I am going to read you a story. Are you sitting comfortably? *Hem-hem. Mi-mi-mi.* 'The Tale of the Failure of Gloster. Once upon a time—'"

"Cut to the chase," said Buddy.

Lou sighed. She loved her *Tales*, but long experience had convinced her that Buddy did not. "OK," she said. "This is the story of a tailor who was a failure. Someone wanted him to make, I dunno, a tracksuit maybe, double quick. But the failure got ill. So the mice came out in the night and finished the tracksuit, and the failure never knew anything about it."

"So what was in it for the mice?" said Buddy.

"Crumbs," said Lou. "The situation was not unlike our own."

Buddy frowned, then nodded. "Got it," he said. He leaned over the board and switched on various microphones. "Gonna be a long night," he said.

Next day, the band trooped into the studio at three p.m. sharp. Enid was in the corner, telephoning.

"Give it another listen," said Fingers, rubbing the sleep out of his eyes.

"That's right," said Kenyatta, yawning.

Eric was loping around the studio, looking for black birds behind the furniture. Igor reached forward. He punched a switch with a finger whose nail seemed to have got longer in the night. Yesterday's dismal recording thundered into the studio air—

"Woooh," said Eric.

The others were sitting up straighter too. Kenyatta McClatter was batting at his forehead, and Fingers Trubshaw was clearing out his ears, and Igor's toothy jaw was hanging open, revealing a great red lolling tongue. Enid's finger hung suspended above the keypad.

Yesterday, the music had been rubbish. Today, it was just absolutely, cosmically spot on. There was a sort of thump in the rhythm section, a thickness in the guitar sound, a sharpness in the riffs . . .

"Good as you ever vas," said Igor. "Yust like the old days."

"We played like that when we was young," said Trubshaw, gazing past a life of lawn care at a rockin' youth.

"Very young," said Kenyatta.

"Hmm," said Enid. "Where are the kids?"

"Sleepin'," said Igor.

"Hmm," said Enid again. "Boys, I know they want this record to be a ravin' success. Oops."

"Raven?" said Eric, his face stark white.

"Not spelled like that."

But it was too late. The green curtains of hair had swished together in front of the face. "Wooooh," said a small, grim voice somewhere in the interior. And all that day, no matter how Fingers and Kenyatta laid down the big truck rhythms and Sid bipped the Spirit Drum, Eric's guitar sounded as if it had wet wool instead of strings.

The band worked until dawn. It was no good. As the moon, now one day away from full, dipped behind the ruined graveyard on the slopes of the mountain, Igor reached out a talon—definitely a talon now—and flipped the OFF switch.

"Bed," said Enid.

They nodded. Gothalinda was waiting in the Hall of Columns. On a table beside her were three gleaming new Stihl chainsaws.

"You vant to cut in half ze furnitures?" she said. "Vill maybe make you feel good?"

"Haven't the heart, somehow," said Trubshaw, not without a loving look at his favorite garden machinery brand.

Kenyatta and Eric shook their heads, their hearts too full for speech.

"Sleep vell, boys," said Gothalinda. The first ray

of dawn pierced the darkness of the hall. "Eek!" she cried. She flitted toward the dark stairs to her bedcrypt.

Death Eric trudged upstairs. The Hall of Columns stood empty, except for the rosy light of early morning . . .

"All clear," said a voice on the stairs.

And down tiptoed Buddy and Lou, past the pond, between the columns, ignoring the chainsaws. They heaved open the soundproof studio door. Buddy switched on the studio board. Lou raided the studio fridge for breakfast. "Ho hum," she said.

"Ho hum," said Buddy. "Failure of Gloster time?"

"Failure of Gloster time it is."

All through the lovely summers day, Castle Bones dreamed in its shadowy gardens. Far beneath the ground in the studio, the Thrashmettle children wove roaring webs of sound. Deep in her cold, cold bed, Gothalinda caught the vibrations and smiled in her unbreathing sleep.

Everything was going to work out fine. She could feel it in her bones.

The band trooped into the studio at three p.m. sharp.

"Give it another listen," said Kenyatta, stretching.

"Sure will," said Trubshaw, rasping his stubble with his thumb.

Eric was on the black bird hunt.

"Ahem," said Igor. "I haf to tell you gentlemens that moonrise is at nine."

"So?"

"Time is short," said Igor, reaching out a finger— a truly *animal* finger now—for the PLAY button.

"What can we do by nine?" said Fingers gloomily.

"Wha?" said Kenyatta.

"Wooooh!" said Eric.

For the playback had begun.

Kenyatta McClatter was cleaning out his ears, and Fingers Trubshaw was batting at his forehead, and Igor's face was split by a wolfish—a *slightly too wolfish*—grin.

"'S, like, *matured* overnight," said Eric.

"Matured?"

"Like wine."

"It's music, not wine," said Fingers, who, like all bassists, was very literal-minded.

"Vocals," said Eric. "We gotta put the vocals on."

Reader, by now you may be lost, and it would be hard to blame you. A word, then, about the techniques of making metal music records in the

148

Early Analog, which is to say totally old-fashioned, studio at Castle Bones. It goes like this. You record a drum track and a bass track and a guitar track, and you lay them on top of each other. Then you maybe lay down more drums and certainly more guitar. Then you mix it up and decide that it is no good. Then Buddy and Lou sneak down while everyone in the house is asleep, and play beautiful bits on keyboards and guitars and strings, and mix them onto the tracks you have. So what was in the studio that afternoon was a red-hot instrumental version of "Where's the Festival?" and "We Are Really Really Lost," without the voices. Feedback metal voices are a problem for children. But the backing track was now so supremely perfect that band morale was tip-top, and one and all were raring to go.

"Voices!" cried Eric, who seemed for the moment to have forgotten the Curse of the Raven.

So out they went into the studio. Enid wrote the words in black felt-tip marker on a sheet of paper so huge that even Eric could not ignore it. Eric sang them, in roughly the right order. Kenyatta took the high harmonies, and Trubshaw took the very high harmonies. It sounded very, very good. And wonder of wonders, Eric was getting right into it.

Too far into it.

"Nearly," he kept saying. "Like, one more take."

And behind the desk, Igor kept looking at the watch on his wrist. His increasingly hairy wrist.

"One more," said Eric.

"Hurry," said Igor. He was scratching himself with his foot and his tongue kept falling out of his jaws.

"Roll 'em," said Eric.

The singing commenced. Enid looked at the calendar on the wall. She looked at the clock, whose second hand was fifteen seconds away from nine o'clock, moonrise. She looked at the singers, who were performing yet another perfectly OK version of "We Are Really Really Lost." It was absolutely fine, except for the screams. The screams were merely OK. An OK scream is a waste of time. The only scream worth having on a feedback metal cut is a totally hellish scream.

Outside the studio's only window, a lightness appeared in the sky. Any second now, the moon would rise. Enid drew breath to say something—

The moon rose.

Igor's ears grew, and his eyes shrank, and his

teeth became huge fangs, and a great tail burst through the seat of his jeans.

It was a terrible sight. Seeing it, Eric let out a scream. It was the kind of scream that stops traffic, breaks glass, and causes birds to fall unconscious from the sky.

It was also the kind of scream that sells a million records. The werewolf that had been Igor sprang at Enid. With a graceful bullfighter's *veronica*, she opened the studio door. Were-Igor landed in the corridor and was gone. Enid pressed the STOP button, rewound, pressed PLAY.

"Wodger think?" she said.

"Far *out*," said everyone.

Next day, Running Dave arrived in his van. He marched into the studio, clamped the earphones on his head, and closed his eyes. Enid pressed the PLAY button. For a second, Dave sat still as a stone.

Then his head began to bang.

It banged some more.

When the music stopped, it was still banging. Banging like a road drill.

"Brilliant!" he cried, once his pupils had stopped

whirling. "Masterful. Fix yourselves a tour!" Then he burst into tears of joy.

Standing to one side, Lou and Buddy discreetly shook hands.

"Thank you, Brothers Grime," said Lou.

"And nice one, Dad," said Buddy. "Nothing can stop us now."

"We shall all live happily ever after and nothing shall stand in our way," said Lou.

Reader, when people say things like this, they are sometimes right and sometimes wrong and sometimes half right.

Nothing shall stand in our way, Lou had said, tempting Fate.

It may be that Fate noticed that when she had said "nothing," she had not said "nobody."

If she had said "nobody," she would have been just plain wrong.

6

That evening, the arches and turrets of Castle
Bones lay sprawled under a large, pale moon in the
Caddy's rearview mirror. There was Gothalinda
waving, radiant in black velvet, holding the silver
chain lead attached to the spiked collar of the wolf
that would be Igor until the moon waned a bit. And
there in the Caddy were the happy faces of Death
Eric, Buddy, and Lou, on their way home with
the new songs in the can. Even before the Caddy
passed between the twin mausoleums at the end of
the drive, Enid was on the phone, steering with her

mighty knees, arranging dates.

After ten minutes she turned. "They're mad for it," she said. "They're paying cash, to us, not Per."

"Who are?"

"The tour venues. The Wheel and Martyr. And the Dark Holler. And a few others."

"The Dark Holler?" said Fingers Trubshaw.

"Are we *worthy*?" said Kenyatta McClatter.

"Rice," said Eric. "I could just fancy a plate of rice."

"Bit of a big gig, the Dark Holler," said Sid the Soothsayer. "I'd be worried, if I were—hey!"

For the Caddy had swerved violently as Enid grabbed him and dragged him into the front seat and covered his face with burning kisses.

"With chicken," said Eric. "Not crow."

He fell into a brooding silence. So did everyone else, or as much of a silence as was possible with six MP3 players going full blast.

"The Dark Holler?" said Buddy, shifting an earpiece.

"I know what the Dark Holler is," said Lou. "But presumably you asked me that question so you could explain, and the reader could sort of eavesdrop."

"Bit tacky."

All right. The Dark Holler had once been a greyhound track. Then it had been a football stadium. Then it had been—

All right, all right. The important thing about the Dark Holler, set as it was on the far outskirts of Smoke City, was that it held half a million people, and it was the funkiest, chainwearingest, headbangingest, airguitarplayingest, crowdsurfingest rock venue on planet Earth. Everybody knew it. Play the Holler well and your career, if off track, was back on track, and the wads of cash came thundering in.

"We could get really fabulous school uniforms then," said Lou, who knew the facts above. "And books. And snakes."

"And scientific instruments beyond the dreams of Newton," said Buddy. "Also bears."

"If they play well," said Enid.

More silence. Bands that did bad gigs at the Holler got torn limb from limb. If they were lucky.

"Orright," said Eric. "So let's go get some warming up done. We're on tour now. No more Mr. Nice Guy. Call the house. Tell the housekeeper to fill up the pool, plus we want a chainsaw in every room."

The happy silence fell again. The lights of Smoke

City crawled up the sky. The limo turned between the huge white marble Costa de Lott gateposts and crunched to a halt on the gravel acres in front of the house. Everyone was wildly excited. The children were riding mountain bikes up and down the double staircase, while from the bedrooms there came the sound of chainsaws and wild laughter.

Enid sat in the kitchen, sipping a moody mug of tea and thinking about lost love. From outside came a whistle, a crash, and an explosion. She looked out of the window; her brooding look changed to an indulgent smile. "First TV in the swimmin' pool," she said. "Happy days."

"Bleep!" cried Flatpick the budgie, delighted to have people to swear at again.

Beside Enid, Sid the Soothsayer smiled as he peered into his tea leaves. "It's gonna be . . . *mph*," he cried as Enid's great hand blocked his mouth.

Consider the facts, though. Death Eric was going on tour to promote their excellent new record. The band would attract vast crowds and be paid spot cash. Per had vanished, but everyone was managing quite nicely without him. What could possibly go wrong?

Wait for it.

*

The house was in sunny mood at breakfast time. Gone were the days of dry bread. The cooks had lashed out. Enid dug into steak, salmon, bacon, eggs, more bacon, hash browns, toast, fried bread, papayas, pineapples, and melon, topped off with a generous layer of brown sauce and maple syrup. Lou and Buddy ate two helpings of cereal, followed by mushroom omelettes of the highest quality, washed down with strawberry milkshakes made with real strawberries.

"Right," said Enid, belching in a gigantic but ladylike manner. "Shopping, anyone? The limo will be at the door in half an hour."

"Ideal," said the children. They strolled down to the Blue Room, where they played *A Small Music for Shortly After Breakfast* by J. S. Brick. As the last notes died away, the kids sat back in their beautiful mahogany chairs, drinking in the complete silence.

"Hist!" said Buddy, raising a finger.

Of course Lou was already listening.

The silence was no longer complete. A very small puttering noise was creeping into the Blue Room. The children looked at each other, wild-eyed.

"Perhaps it's a lawn mower," said Lou brightly,

hoping against hope.

Buddy shook his head with a deep, deep weariness. "It sounds to me like a French car. A small one."

"Oh," said Lou.

For a moment, there was only the engine noise, getting louder. Then Lou and Buddy got up and opened the Blue Room door and gazed across the lawn to the front drive.

A saffron-yellow Citroën 2CV was *put-putt*ing slowly across the gravel. It stopped. A door opened. A tall figure wearing an orange sari got out, went down on its knees, and stuck its nose into the gravel.

"She is kissing the ground," said Lou, her green eyes narrow.

"Means she's here to stay," said Buddy, heavy brows low over his deep-set eyes.

"Hmm," said both children, like depressed bees. They walked across the lawn to the little car.

The woman in the sari turned to look at them. Her eyes were very wide open and there was a small red palm tree painted on her forehead above the join of her eyebrows. She was amazingly thin.

"Hello, Mum," said the children, smiling hopefully.

The eyes rolled back in the head. "Ing ang bing bang shangalang," chanted the mouth. "Children!"

"That's us," said Buddy.

Lou did not even speak.

It was going to be like that again.

Their mother had bent forward. At first Lou thought she was going to kiss them, and cheered up. But there was no puckering of lips, just sniffing.

"Breathe," said their mother.

Lou and Buddy obeyed. They had to, or suffocate.

"Argh!" cried their mother sharply, recoiling in a flutter of sari.

"Wha?"

"There is bacon in the air!" cried Wave, in a high, keening voice. "The cry of unborn animals!"

("Eggs," said Buddy.)

"The shrieks of roots ripped from the earth!"

("Mushrooms," said Lou. "We didn't have carrots.")

But Wave was not listening. "Is this what I find?" she cried. "I come back from a few months' meditation and find my house polluted with the flesh of animals slain in anger?"

"Not anger, exactly," said Buddy, feeling at a disadvantage.

"And mostly vegetables," said Lou, unsure of her

ground.

The long hennaed hand patted them on their heads. "Little ones, you understand so little," said their mother. "But I will reveal it for you. Now, come into the house and we will get you out of these nasty blazers and trousers and skirts and into lovely orange robes, and you will be little Sanyasins and know Bliss!"

"We'd rather know English Literature," said Lou.

"And Math," said Buddy.

Their mother gave a laugh that tinkled like temple bells. "All is maya," she cried. "What you in your simple fashion call Illusion. I have come to teach you the ways of the Void. Follow me, disciples!" She swept into the house.

"Actually," said Buddy to her back, "we see ourselves more as your children than as your disciples."

But Wave's nostrils were twitching to the fumes of fillet steak wafting from the kitchen, so she paid no attention to the little people following her.

There was a bit of a scene in the kitchen. This was caused by Wave flinging the meat in the pans out of the window, followed by the contents of the fridge and the freezer. Lou did not want to go in, but Buddy stuck his head around the door.

"She is talking to a beet," he said. "She is telling it that she knows exactly how it feels. She is mentioning to it that from now on we are going to drink only spring water. We will eat only whole grains that have fallen naturally from the plant, not been ripped from the ear by the violent hand of the farmer."

There was the crash of breaking glass and the fire alarm went off and Flatpick the budgie started swearing. It was an extra-loud fire alarm. Rock stars' usually are, what with there being a lot of chainsaw fuel and highly flammable tattoo inks about the place, and people sleeping at all hours. Within three minutes, all nine of the house's occupants were in the drive, plus four small fans who had parachuted into the attic in 1994 and had been camping out there ever since. There was a lot of eye rubbing. Eric was wearing a spider-silk sarong, and the night bear tattooed on his back seemed to blink in the unaccustomed light. Fingers Trubshaw was wearing striped flannel pajamas, and Kenyatta McClatter an elegant paisley dressing gown with quilted lapels. They all milled around, bumping into each other and saying "Where's the fire?" and "Wha?" except Eric, who was peering about him, presumably seeking birds of ill omen.

Wave snapped her fingers. "Stepladder!" she said curtly to Enid.

Enid fetched a stepladder, her large face resembling a huge, beautiful landscape becoming aware that there would soon be an earthquake.

"Here," said Wave, pointing at a good stepladder site on the gravel. "Megaphone."

"You don't need a megaphone," said Enid.

Wave opened her mouth to make a spiritual remark, saw that what Enid had said was quite true, and climbed the ladder. "AHEM," she said, to attract everyone's attention.

Everyone looked at her.

"I am BACK," said Wave.

"Orange," said Eric. "She's orange, not black."

"Not *black*, *back*."

"Wha?"

"WELL," said Wave. "I turn my back for a mere eleven months and thirty days and WHAT DO I FIND?"

"Not much, really—," said Eric.

"I find ANARCHY. KARMIC DISASTER. Vegetables ripped untimely from their MOTHER EARTH. The breath of my children polluted with POOR SCREAMING, er, EGGS. Not to mention the muscles of DEAD ANIMALS being CALLOUSLY SCORCHED in the kitchen."

"Really?" said Eric, his interest roused. "Like, a nice steak?"

"Peace, gormandizer. I have DESTROYED IT ALL." She swept the horrified faces of her audience with a laser eye. "And the roadies tell me you are going on tour. Well! It seems I have arrived in the nick of time!" She plunged her hand into the bosom of her sari and came up with a sheet of paper. "Here is your timetable."

"Table?" said Eric. "Time?"

"Cast your eyes over it," said Wave, ignoring him. "Eight hours' yoga a day is a nice, easy way in. And there is a rota for drawing water from the spring and waiting by blades of grass for the seeds to fall out." She smiled, a wide smile, completely barmy. "Any questions?"

"Small one," said Fingers Trubshaw.

Wave spread her hands. "Ask and it shall be given, my child."

"Yur," said Fingers. "Only, seeing as we got a tour, what about the music?"

"Ah, music, my worldly one," said Wave, now in

a distinct North Indian accent. "Is it not truly said, it is learning to learn that is the greatest learning?"

"Come again?" said Fingers.

"Clean out yer ears, blockhead!" shrieked Wave, who had a short fuse for a spiritual person. "What I mean is, if you do exactly what I tell you, everything will work out just the way I planned."

"So no playing, then," said Kenyatta.

"Playing will not be necessary. Soundwaves are an intrusion on the air. How would you like it if something sent waves through you and made you wobble? Plus it is bad karma for our brothers and sisters the wasps and mosquitoes and similar. I shall be in the Blue Room in ten minutes, dispensing wisdom. Class, dis-MISSED!"

"But that's our music room," said Lou.

"Not anymore it isn't," snarled Wave.

Everyone turned up. Wave was a powerful character. Once Wave had decided on something, that was that. Even Buddy and Lou went.

"Right!" said Wave. She was now dressed in orange tights, and her eyes looked in two separate directions. "On the count of three. Yogic exercises. BEGIN!"

First they stood on their left leg, and Eric fell over

to the right. Then they stood on their right leg, and Eric fell over to the left. Then they stood on their heads, and Eric fell over in all directions. Then they sat cross-legged. After five minutes, Eric began to snore. Wave clapped a Japanese rice flail next to his ear and he fell over again.

During the meditation, Lou had been edging cross-legged closer to the back of the room, and Buddy had been edging after her. They waited until Wave's eyes had rolled back in her head. Then they made the final dash out of the door and into the shrubbery. Here they sat on garden chairs made of old guitars and waited for the parts of themselves that had gone to sleep to wake up.

"What do you reckon?" she said.

"Bad. They're meant to be, you know, warming up for the tour. Playing and breaking up rooms and getting psyched up. As it is, they're getting psyched down."

"Perhaps she'll stop."

"Probably not," said Buddy.

"No." Lou unbuttoned the pocket in which she kept her *Tales from the Brothers Grime*. "She is only one woman," she said.

"A very mad one."

"Exactly. Buddy, I am going to read you a story. 'Once upon a time—'"

"Cut to the chase."

"OK. It is about a frog and a bus. The frog reckoned it could be as big as the bus. The bus was getting really sick of this bigheaded frog giving it the verbal, so it said, 'Here's a bicycle pump. If you blow yourself up, you will be just as big as me.' Then it drove off."

"And?" said Buddy, interested in spite of himself.

"The frog pumped himself up until he exploded. *Splat*. All over the landscape. No more trouble from *him*."

"You are going to give her a bicycle pump?" said Buddy.

"In a manner of speaking."

"What manner?"

"Easy," said Lou, her green eyes taking on the old dangerous glitter. "She will soon become involved with the Amalgamated Orphans of Hongania."

"What is Hongania?"

"A very, very long way away, and that is all you need to know. Now, we have some telephoning to do."

*

The yoga class broke for lunch at one o'clock. The band lurched out, groaning and holding on to bits of themselves that were bruised, stretched, or twisted. The only person in reasonable shape was Enid, who had managed to have a refreshing doze in the back row. And, of course, Wave, who wore a large white smile slung under her madly glowing blue eyes.

Buddy and Lou were waiting outside, hands joined, smiling inscrutably.

"The noon grains are served," said Lou. "And we got the spring water."

"Wha?" said Eric, hobbling.

"Lunchtime," said Buddy, translating.

"Far *out*," said Eric, sniffing the air. "I'm, like, *starving*."

The kitchen table was laid for ten. Incense burned in holders down the middle. Wave sat at the head of the table, Eric at the foot, everyone else in between. It had been a hard morning and everyone was hungry.

There was silence, except for sneezing caused by the incense. Finally Eric said, "What's for lunch, then?"

Buddy pointed to a dish in the middle of the

table. On the dish was a brownish mound, which steamed faintly. "That," he said.

"Grains," said Wave. "Beautiful."

"Oh," said Eric.

There was a stirring from the corner of the kitchen. Flatpick the budgie had just caught sight of the pile on the table. "Bleep," said Flatpick, deeply moved. "Get your cotton-picking hands off my lunch."

"Woooh," said Eric, contemplating his birdseed. "Is this it?"

"No, no!" cried Lou heartily. "There is spring water, too!" She picked up a wholesome earthenware jug from the sideboard and walked around the table.

Wave nodded. "It is very right that the young disciples should serve their olders."

"Whaddyamean, old?" said Kenyatta.

"And wisers," said Wave hastily.

"It would be wise not to eat this filf," said Fingers.

"Bleep!" cried Flatpick.

"Water, madam?" said Lou.

"Mmm!" said Wave, beaming.

When Lou poured, the water did not so much trickle out of the jug as fall out in a greenish lump.

Wave was so busy beaming healthily down the table that she did not have a chance to look at her glass before she took a huge energy-giving sip. "Mmmargh," she said.

"You got grass on your teef," said Kenyatta.

"Duckweed," said Fingers Trubshaw.

"I wanna beer, dear," said Eric, getting right to the point for the first time in his life.

"Ha bleeping ha!" cried Flatpick.

"Put a cloth over that," said Eric.

"I poured all the beer down the drain," said Wave, munching a spoonful of birdseed one hundred times. "I can just *feel* the energy building."

"I can feel the hunger building," said Kenyatta. He flipped out a mobile phone and dialed a number. "Roger?" he said. "Of Roger's Champion Burgers? We want, what, ten, no make that nine of your Big Burgers. Pure beef only, low fat, Roquefort dressing, salad, sesame buns, extra ketchup. The roadie will be round in—"

Long hennaed fingers snatched the phone from his hand. "That order is cancelled!" cried Wave, and slammed it shut. "*Honestly!*"

"I am not a budgie," said Kenyatta sulkily.

"Nor me," said Fingers.

"Nor us," growled the roadies.

"Bleep!" cried Flatpick from under his cloth.

"Guys! Guys!" said Eric, sensing a slight disturbance in the vibe.

"It is a matter of getting used to a correct diet," said Wave, sipping water and discreetly spitting out pondweed. "I am going to wait by an ear of corn all afternoon, so you will have to do without me."

"Oh," said Kenyatta, looking very cheerful.

"Dearie, dearie me," said Trubshaw, grinning broadly.

"*Great*, darlin'," said Eric as the message finally got through. "Oops."

"Not at all," said Wave, spreading her hands and giving a Mother Goddess smile.

"I mean, we can do some music. Oops!"

"But you can, you can!" cried Wave. "Of a noninterruptive type that will love the air and massage the mosquitoes! Look what I have got for you!" She clapped her hands. Two junior roadies scuttled into the room, carrying a big packing case. "Open up," she cried.

They opened up. Everyone gathered around and looked inside. Jaws dropped and swung, creaking.

"Wha?" said Eric.

"Sitars," said Trubshaw.

"One sitar. One sarod. One set of tabla. Now you can play spiritual raga."

"Wait, guys," said Eric. "Let's—"

"We play metal music," said Kenyatta. "*Feedback* metal."

"On these," said Wave.

"Wooooh, darlin'," said Eric, agonized. "No can do!"

"Can too. Pick 'em up. Wrong way up, Fingers."

"Oh."

"A-one, two, *three*."

The kitchen filled with a noise like cats fighting in a grandfather clock. It collapsed in a loud rumble.

"Nice drumming," said Fingers.

"That was me stomach, man," said Kenyatta glumly.

Wave chucked her chin in the air, took a raffia basket from the wall, and left. Lou uncovered Flatpick, who began to swear horribly, but not as horribly as everyone else in the room.

Everyone except Eric.

"Oi," said Eric.

"She goes or we go," said Kenyatta and Fingers.

"Ahem," said Buddy, breaking off the conversation

he was having with Lou and putting his wrists together, miming handcuffs.

"So put me in jail."

"True," said Kenyatta.

Eric was sitting up very straight. "No way," he said. "I am old-fashioned about these things. What my baby wants, my baby gets. I will brook no opposition. Got any more of that birdseed?"

Flatpick the budgie led the swearing again.

Lou noticed that nobody had yet left. "Ahem," she said. "I have got an idea."

"A good one," said Buddy.

Six furious faces and one huge kindly one, belonging to Enid, turned upon them.

"Yes, children?" said Enid.

"How do you feel about orphans?" said Lou.

It had been a tough afternoon and Wave was eager for her mu tea. She had waited by an ear of corn and caught five kernals, though she had had a bit of a quarrel with a bird over the last one, and the bird had won, so that left only four. She could not get rid of the idea that four kernals of corn were not going to go far between ten people. She tried meditating, but the facts remained the same. So she went to

SELFRODS and tried shopping, and that worked better, so she bought quite a lot of clothes on account, and a five-pound bag of lentils from the Food Hall. Then she snapped at Thick Rick, who was driving the limo, to take her back to Dunravin.

She sank into the cushions and tried to feel confident. It was hard to get the energy flow going. She was actually a bit nervous about Death Eric and its metal energy. They made her feel small. She needed to make a big gesture, so she would be doing *enough*. A really *big* gesture that would make her bigger. Like running the tour. "Yes!" she cried, clapping her hands very quietly. That was *it*! She would run the tour! And they would *have* to do what she said!

Reader, you will have noticed that this thought process is not unlike that of the Frog in "The Tale of the Frog and the Bus."

Wait for it.

As the limousine turned in at the gates of Dunravin, Wave was surprised to see a large banner stretched from gate pillar to gate pillar. On it was printed ADVANCE GUARD FOR THE AMALGAMATED ORPHANS OF HONGANIA RELIEF

Oo, thought Wave. Womanwave. Really, really *me*!

The limo rounded the last corner. Wave was amazed to see dozens of people standing on the gravel. When they saw the limo, they started to cheer. Wave had no idea what was going on, but these people obviously loved her, so she went all warm and pink and began to feel much bigger again.

The limo stopped. Someone opened the door for her and she stepped gracefully out.

"Wave!" the crowd chanted. "O Wave, all mother and all-around excellent person, greetings and congratulations!"

Wave stood and put her hands together and did namastes left and right and tried to look as if she did not think she deserved all this. From the corner of her eye she noticed Buddy and Lou, out of their saris and once again dressed in their rather severe school uniform–type clothes.

"Little ones!" she cried, folding them in her bony arms and hoping someone was taking a picture.

"Good afternoon," they said politely.

"All this for me?" she said.

"It is no more than your due," said Lou.

"As you know," said Buddy. "In your wisdom, that is."

"Yes." Wave was not quite sure what was real and what was not. She was definitely feeling bigger, though. "And . . . er . . . Hongania."

"Poor Hongania," said Lou, shaking her head sadly.

"Particularly the orphans," said Buddy, shaking his head too.

"I have always felt a really positive energy about the Honganian orphans," said Wave. "But—"

"Hoorah!" cried Buddy and Lou.

"Hoorah!" cried the crowd of people.

Around the corner, there came a bus. It was a small bus, white. Along its side it said GRAND HONGANIAN BENEFIT TOUR—ADVANCE PARTY.

"Wha—," said Wave.

"Ssh!" said Lou, digging her in the ribs with a heavily bony energy.

Wave noticed that a small fat man was standing in front of her. Under his arm was a black cocked hat with white ostrich feathers. The parts of his chest and stomach not smothered in gold braid were dotted with medals. "Madam!" he cried.

"Who are you?" said Wave.

"The Honganian Ambassador," hissed Buddy.

"Oo," said Wave, who despite her yogic ideas was a sucker for a uniform.

"Madam, on behalf of the people of Hongania, I thank you for your promised help," said the Ambassador.

"Help?" said Wave. "But—"

"It will be a journey of many veeks," said the Ambassador. "The roads are bad, the plumbing atrocious. But I know you are not givink a fig or monkeys for comfort. You vill hav a varm Honganian velcom and all the grains you can stuff down. Und the help of our monarch, King Vlad the Remorseless! Brave woman, farewell!"

"Off already, Ambassador?" said Wave, dazed.

"It's you," hissed Buddy, pushing her toward the white bus.

Wave would have pushed back, but a great cheer went up, and she felt a size bigger, and it would have shrunk her to struggle.

"Your task is to find suitable spots for benefit concerts in aid of orphans," he said. "With positive energy and stuff like that."

"Ooer," said Wave, on the step of the bus.

"The telephones in Hongania are not great and the Ambassador says something seems to be eating the postmen," said Lou. "So we have packed you some carrier pigeons."

"Off you go," said Buddy. "Thick Rick will be your driver. He has his orders. Good luck!"

Wave turned on the bus steps and thought of doing a runner into the house. But everyone cheered and yelled, "Speech!" and she felt absolutely huge. "Energy!" she said. "Positive! I shall cherish the orphans, and if you obey my orders exactly, they will become rich!"

"Hoorah!" cried the crowd, and it surged forward, knocking her up the steps and into the bus. Someone slammed the door. Thick Rick trod on the accelerator. The bus roared away in the direction of the Channel ports. As it rounded the corner, the cheering stopped.

"Thank you, everyone!" cried Enid. "Please place your costumes in the box. Careful with that hat, Ambassador."

"Sorry," said the Ambassador, taking off his coat and revealing under it a T-shirt that said AVIS RENTACROWD—WE SHOUT LOUDER. "So where exactly is Hongania?"

"Dunno," said Enid. "Other side of Russia somewhere."

"Phew," said Lou and Buddy. "So now let us cook some steaks and get on with it. The first gig is the day after tomorrow."

And on with it they got.

7

Two days later, after tea, Enid and the children and the road crew held a strategy meeting.

"Wheel and Martyr gig tonight. From now on, nothing must go wrong," said Buddy, frowning deeply.

"Our uniforms depend on it," said Lou.

"And our scientific instruments. Lou, can you report on how everyone is feeling?"

"With pleasure. You will be pleased to hear that, while retaining his interest in lawn care, Fingers can now spend a good long time without so much as thinking about lawn mowers and fertilizer. Kenyatta is still a keen fish fryer, but he does it in the privacy of his own room, and I have a feeling that he is beginning to prefer his drum kit to his lard. And Dad is deeply committed, like always, dear Dad."

"Excellent," said Buddy. "Enid, your department?"

"Everything's ready. Promoters, publicity, extra road crew hired, gear, stage clothes, bat colony, fruit juice. The Wheel and Martyr as a warm-up. Then it's the big one."

"Dark Holler?" said Lou.

"Correct."

"Make or break," said Buddy.

"It'll be fine," said Sid the Soothsayer.

There was the slapping noise of three heads being buried in six hands. The room filled with the distant chug of Death Eric practicing. Gradually the heads came up again. The band was playing "Donkey" with exceptional skill and correctness.

Then Eric's guitar made a noise like a wildcat doing push-ups on a red-hot stove. The wildcat became a space rocket. The space rocket exploded.

There was silence.

The children looked around them in amazement.

Always sensitive to the first hint of trouble, Enid had already picked up a heavy object in each hand and was sprinting out of the door. Buddy and Lou went after her.

Fingers and Kenyatta were standing outside the practice pavilion.

"What happened?" said Enid.

"Vanished," said Kenyatta.

"What, in a puff of smoke style of thing?"

"Nah," said Fingers. "Bird came in through the window. Eric looked at its foot. Then he done a runner."

"Its *foot*?" said Lou.

"Nasty-looking bird."

"A raven?" said Buddy.

"Not that black. More like black*ish*."

"And then?" Enid began to look threatening, in a beautiful kind of way.

"He unrolled a bit of paper off its leg," Fingers said.

"And then?"

"He read it and dropped it."

"And then?"

"He sort of freaked and went out of the window. Took him two tries."

"And what was on the bit of paper?"

"I picked it up. Take a look." Kenyatta passed a tiny rolled-up bit of paper to Enid.

Enid unrolled it. It was printed, apparently with a potato. GREETINGS FROM HONGANIA, it said. VEATHER IS HERE. VISH YOU VERE LOVELY. ORGANIZING SPIRITUALLY NICE VENUES. OM SHANTI WOMANWAVE.

"Whassa problem?" said Enid.

"Ahem," said Lou, pointing.

In the bottom right-hand corner of the printed postcard was a stylized picture of a black bird with two heads, each bearing a beady red eye.

"The two-headed raven," said Lou.

"Crest of the Mountain Kingdom of Hongania," said Buddy.

Silence fell. Into the silence came a sound like a deathwatch beetle chewing its way through a doorpost.

"Over here," said Lou.

Off they marched into the shrubbery until they came to the trunk of a mighty oak tree.

"This is it," said Buddy.

"How do you know?"

"The ladder leaning against it is a clue." Red dust

was filtering down through the air. "Plus I think there is a witch doctor up there."

From up in the dense green canopy of the tree came the tap of fingers on a drum. An angry cawing grew louder, as if there were many birds with a lot on their minds.

Buddy sighed, then climbed up the ladder and into the tree, following the noise through leaves and branches. Suddenly he found himself in a high fork, bathed in leaf-green sunlight. It was a nice place. It would have been nicer if it had not contained Sid the Soothsayer, painted dark red, perched on a branch, tapping a drum. It would have been nicer still if there had not been about forty rooks sitting around in a circle shouting at something in their hoarse rooky voices. And it would have been just about perfect if on top of the problems aforementioned, in the middle of the rooks, curled up in a nest of twigs, there had not been the lanky, green-haired figure of Eric Thrashmettle, his father.

"Dad," said Buddy, waving his hand at a rook that seemed hungry for his shoelaces. "What are you *doing*?"

"Relaxin'," said Eric.

"Ahem," said Sid.

"Oh yeah. Plus Sid here said I should get to the middle of this black-bird problem and explain it to them and maybe they would stop. So as I was saying, bird guys, I am really sorry if I done you, like, wrong, and naturally I will do anything I can to sort it out. Like tickets for the Dark Holler gig? Backstage like passes or maybe you'll just fly in anyway, ha ha. Guys?"

The rooks gazed upon him, tilting their heads from side to side.

Buddy said, "This curse business is a lot of fuss about nothing."

"Oi!" said Sid the Soothsayer. "I went on a course."

Eric did not seem to hear. He said to Buddy, "You reckon?"

"I'm sure."

Eric stood up, brushing bits of twig from his leather T-shirt. "Oh, well, in that case," he said, and stepped out of the nest.

There was a thin, fading scream, a crackle of branches, and a thud.

"See? No man can defy Fate," said Sid the Soothsayer, baring his filed teeth.

But Buddy was not there to listen. He had gone

down the tree like a fireman going down a pole. The people at the bottom were standing around what had once been an incredibly rare rhododendron bush. In the midst of the wreckage, a spidery figure groaned and stirred.

"Dad?" said Lou.

The red spectacles turned toward her. "What place is this?" said the voice of Eric Thrashmettle.

"You are in the woods," said Lou, in slow, consoling tones. "You have just had a small accident—"

"Wooh," said Eric, clutching his head and rising shakily to his feet. "'S all coming back. I, like, went to try to make friends with the black birds and they, like, double hexed me and threw me out of the tree."

"You walked," said Buddy.

"Same thing," said Eric. "Woooh."

There was a noise like a small hand grenade exploding in a bucket of petrol.

"Honestly!" said Lou. "This is the limit! You jump out of trees and blame the wrong kind of birds for pushing you! Now, would you mind stopping making this silly fuss and concentrating on your music so Buddy and I can go back to school and get top marks in everything."

"Wooh," said Eric. *"Dangerous."* And he walked away, shaking his head.

Enid said, "The only person who could tell him that kind of thing was Per."

Lou looked guilty. "Silly of me," she said.

There was a crash twenty yards away in the wood. "Sorry, man," said Eric to the beech tree with which he had just collided.

"Give me strength," said Lou.

"You know what?" said Buddy. "I think we ought to go and have a chat with Per."

"How are we supposed to find him if Enid can't?"

"Leave that to me," said Buddy, with an air of deepest mystery.

"Oh, very enigmatic," said Lou, her green eyes glinting with sarcasm. "Now, if you have a moment, Sherlock, we have work to do."

The Wheel and Martyr was a public house built in the days when quite a lot of the British Navy wanted to drink beer all at once in the same place. The Navy is not as thirsty as it once was, but the Wheel still stood, a huge, grim shed in a car park full of puddles. The only nice thing about it was on the front, where a huge sign flashed on and off. TONITE

ONLY, said the sign. THE RETURN OF DEATH ERIC.

"Nice," said Enid to the children, who were with her in the lead truck. When you have been a roadie for a few years, you do not worry about the architecture, as long as they have put the right name in lights.

"Yes," said the children, in rather small voices.

"Nice," said Eric, leaning forward in his special swivel chair. *"Cool."* This was the most positive thing he had said for months, and the hearts of all beat high and warm. Then he said, "Woooh," put his hands over his spectacles, and slumped back in his seat.

"Wha?" said Enid, wrestling the big truck over the potholes of the car park.

"Up there," said the children.

And there, wheeling in the storm-wrack racing down the wind above the crazy chimneys of the Wheel, was something that might have been a scrap of burned paper or a kite.

Except that it was neither.

It was a black bird.

"Oh, for goodness' *sake*," said Lou and Buddy, both at once.

"Dad," said Lou, fixing him with her hypnotic

green gaze, "you have cut some great tracks, raven or no raven."

"You think so?" said Eric, blushing.

"So you are going to play a great gig, black bird or no black bird." She squeezed his hand.

"Yeah," said Eric, only half convinced.

There was a jolt of brakes. Roadies hurled themselves out of the truck and started slamming stacks of speakers into puddles. Death Eric had arrived at the Wheel and Martyr.

Normally, the roadies put up the towers of gear while the band relaxed and got into the vibe. Today, the gear went up all right, but the band seemed tense and nervous. The dressing room was about the size of a lavatory but smelled worse. Previous performers had scratched their names in the purple paint on the walls. Down one side was a table with bottles, chocolates, and cages—

Cages?

Sorry. Dear reader, as you probably know, to get an artist to perform at your venue, you give them a contract, in which the artist agrees to perform and you agree to pay them a certain amount when they have done it. You also agree to provide stuff for their enjoyment in the dressing room. Lynda Quayle,

R&B diva, demands a basket of adorable kittens, minimum number nine. Rod Bucket, garage rocker, demands a gallon of lemon-scented brake fluid for reasons he refuses to go into. Death Eric demands gallons of pop, a lot of crisps, one cage of vampire bats, and one cage of snakes, assorted nonvenomous.

Lou and Buddy took a look into the dressing room and decided it was too small and too smelly. They found themselves at the back of the stage, between the huge speaker cabinets and some black curtains that smelled of beer and cigarettes. A large figure in a print dress was sticking cables to the floor with gaffer tape.

"Oh," said Enid, for it was she. "How's it going?"

"Medium," said Lou.

"We don't like the atmosphere," said Buddy. "We think they're going to play garbage."

"And I have been thinking," said Lou, her hand stealing to the special pocket in her blazer, "of a tale from the Brothers Grime."

Buddy looked ostentatiously at his watch. "Goodness, is that the time already?" he said, and would have left if Enid had not attached an iron hand to his arm.

"Ahem," said Lou, moving into a small pool of

green stagelight. "The story in question is entitled 'Crumplestilts.'" She riffled the well-thumbed pages. "It goes like this. 'Once upon a time—'"

"Cut to the chase," said Buddy.

"If you insist. Well. A wicked king gave a beautiful maiden a shed full of pigs and told her to turn them into racing greyhounds, or someone would be along to chop off her head. Naturally she got into quite a state. When she came round from a bout of weeping, she was surprised to see by her side a gnome with a nose as long as his leg. His name turned out to be Crumplestilts, and he offered to do the job."

"For free?" said Buddy.

"No," said Lou. "But that is not the point. The point is that while the beautiful maiden slept, Crumplestilts did the job on the pigs, and the next morning the barking of the greyhounds was the loudest thing in the land after the king's cries of joy."

There was silence. "So?" said Buddy.

"The audience is king," said Lou. "Small people will help it get what it wants."

"What's in it for the small people?" said Buddy.

"Scientific instruments," said Lou. "Uniforms. Money."

"Ah," said Buddy. "Are you suggesting that we are Crumplestilts, and Death Eric is the beautiful maiden?"

"Precisely. We need the Big Cab."

Five minutes later, a huge speaker was being wheeled onto the stage by ten sweating roadies. This was the Big Cab.

"Cor," said a smooth voice. "Big."

"Yes," said Buddy, turning to fix the new arrival with a lowering eye. "Who are you?"

"Colin de Weasel," said the man. He was tall and muscular, dressed in an ironed T-shirt and ironed jeans. He was wearing dark glasses that made him look like a suntanned insect. "I am the promoter. That means I book the bands and put up the posters and take the money on the door."

"And pay the bands," said Buddy.

"'Course, sonny," said Mr. de Weasel with a false, patronizing smile. "Now then, you and greeneyes run along, because the grown-ups have things they need to make happen."

The children gave Mr. de Weasel smiles of piercing sweetness. "Of course!" they cried, and scampered away.

Once they were around the corner, they stopped scampering and sat down on a cable drum, looking grim.

"Sonny!" said Lou.

"Greeneyes!" said Buddy.

"Ironed jeans," said Lou. "Yuck."

"Told us stuff we already knew," said Buddy. "Needs watching."

Lou sighed. "Ah, well," she said. "Work to do."

"Goodnights first."

They put their heads around the dressing-room door. Kenyatta was sitting in the corner, frying a small plaice on a camping stove. Fingers was crouched over a geranium he was nursing back to health. Eric was in leather stage trousers and Lycra stage top, with a snake wrapped around his neck.

"Night-night!" cried the children, waving.

"'Night," said the band. They sounded subdued.

"Wave to the kids," said Eric to the snake.

The snake hissed a bit and was still.

"Wave," said Eric.

"It can't," said Lou.

"Being a snake," said Buddy. "No arms."

"Oh," said Eric, yawning. "Yeah." He did not sound convinced. "'Night, then, kids."

Buddy closed the door.

"Well," said Lou. "Did they strike you as riders at the gates of Hell who take no prisoners?"

"More like people who've been down so long it feels like up to them," said Buddy.

"Exactly."

They walked down the back of the row of huge speaker cabinets that stretched from side to side of the stage like a street of terraced houses. They stopped in front of the Big Cab. This one really did look like a house. Some waggish person had attached a red door to it. The door had a knocker, and a brass number 13 screwed to a panel.

"Almost looks real," said Buddy.

"Ha ha," said Lou.

She took a key from her pocket, unlocked the door, and went in. Buddy followed.

Inside the Big Cab there was no speaker. Instead, there were a couple of bunks, a keyboard, two guitars, and a large mixing board, with thick leads coiling into the outside world. Above the desk was a CCTV screen, showing views in front of and behind the stage.

"Right," said Lou. "How long?"

"An hour and a half," said Buddy. "Plus obviously

half an hour for compulsory rock 'n'roll lateness."

"Well," said Lou, "I think I could manage a nap." Swinging her feet onto the bunk, she was instantly asleep.

Buddy sat at the mixing board and brought up the set list on the computer. He tuned the guitars. Then he sat at the keyboard, summoned up a harpsichord tinkle, put on some earphones and played himself Snark's *Small Meditations for Long Boring Wait*. A support band went on stage and wriggled and screamed. Actually they were not bad, but Buddy had things on his mind.

His sister was a brilliant girl and her love of the *Tales of the Brothers Grime* certainly came in very useful. But Buddy's mind was a razor-sharp surgical instrument, able to slice into a situation and find out exactly where the problems lay. For some time now he had been gently dismantling the peculiar things that had happened to Death Eric. One thing had led to another. The facts had formed a pattern. Until tonight there had been only one part of the pattern missing. Now the missing part was staring him in the face, and its name was Colin de Weasel. The pattern was complete.

The crowd would have finished arriving. The

house was full; the ticket office would be closing.

He played the final twiddly bit and chord of the *Meditations*. His fingers went to the joystick of the CCTV camera. He pointed the lens at the back of the hall and zoomed in.

Dim shapes moved on the screen—nobody he recognized. "Hangyou," said a voice on the stage. "Hangyou, hangyou. Laze and gemmen, less hearitfor THE GORILLA BROTHERS." The support band grinned and bowed and hoped it would get an encore. But the audience was there for Death Eric, not support bands, so the applause died quickly.

On the CCTV screen a familiar figure came out of the box-office door. It was wearing ironed jeans. It was Colin de Weasel. He was moving through the crowd with a tense, possessive scowl on his face. In his hand he carried a suitcase that looked about the right size and full to the brim. Buddy tracked him through the crowd with sensitive movements of the joystick. De Weasel stopped in front of a door that said PRIVATE. He looked left and right. Then he and the suitcase vanished through the door.

Buddy picked up a small walkie-talkie and murmured into it. Enid's voice came back to him loud and clear. Buddy made certain suggestions.

"Check, darling," said Enid.

Buddy watched the screen long enough to see the large figures of two Death Eric roadies stroll out of the crowd and take up their stations on either side of the door marked PRIVATE. Then he woke his sister. "Five minutes," he said.

Lou yawned, stretched, picked up a guitar and played a lick. "Ready when they are," she said.

Four minutes and fifty seconds later, the hall went black as night. Then it appeared to be struck by lightning several times. From the PA speakers came the sound of racing cars racing and cows mooing, hugely amplified. Behind the cars and the cows a guitar started to feed back. Green smoke billowed from the wings and met in the middle. In front of the smoke there appeared a lanky demon dressed in red. The demon clutched a microphone. "LAZE AN GEMMEN!" it cried in the voice of Norbert Kidney, prominent Smoke City DJ and insider. "WHEELINMARTYR PROULY PRENTS. DEATH—"

KAJOOOOOMMMGGGOWWWWWWNNNN, went the feedback.

"—ERIC!"

OWWWWWWWWWWWWWWWWWWWWWWW,
went the feedback. A flock of bats flittered across
the lights.

And away went the band, into the first mighty
chords of "Apocalypse? Wow!"

Kenyatta was not feeling good. There was something
wrong with the vibe again. Between the golden
flying saucers of his cymbals, the lights and the
crowd throbbed and pulsed. Behind him, Fingers's
bass thudded away like a doomdozer at full throttle.
Not *quite* full throttle, though. And Eric's guitar was
. . . OK. No *more* than OK, though. It was as if
everyone had milk and water in their veins instead
of fire and blood. Talking about fire, thought
Kenyatta, his attention straying from the task at
hand . . . If only he had a tin drum of boiling lard
instead of that floor tom. That was the thing about
cooking. It was consoling. You were either doing it
or not.

"Two, three, *four*," said Buddy in the Big Cab.

Kenyatta noticed a strange thing. All of a sudden,
the sounds got deeper and darker and thicker. And
the groove came together, *thunk*.

Almost, thought Kenyatta, as if there were a couple of extra people in the band.

Fingers Trubshaw was not feeling all that good either. There was something wrong with the vibe again. His mind was partly on the mighty thump of his bass, but mostly on that poor ill geranium he had left in the dressing room. It was an amazingly lovable little thing, but he did not know if he could save it. Fingers's fingers plucked away at the strings of the Precision. But his mind floated in faraway gardens, mowing stripes straight as arrows across lawns of brightest green. He knew he should be right into the music. But he wasn't, and that was that. The band was playing. But it was not playing *together* . . .

"Two, three, *four*," said Buddy in the Big Cab.

Fingers noticed a strange thing. All of a sudden, the musical stew got deeper and darker and thicker. Fingers's mind flew back from his lawns and into the music. And the groove came together, *thunk*.

Almost, thought Fingers, as if there were a couple of extra people in the band.

Eric was not feeling good. Like, really, really double plus ungood. There were a lot of people out there.

The lights were in his eyes. His fingers were whizzing around Rabid Dingo all right, and he could hear someone singing and he was pretty sure the someone was him, but his mind was not in it. His mind was out there behind the glare of the lights, floating among the bats in the rusty iron rafters of the Wheel and Martyr. Not looking at the bats, though. Looking for the sinister, perched shape of a bird a foot long, black as night, with eyes that like looked *through* you and said, Nevermore . . .

Time to sing another verse. Time to adjust the snake on his neck. After the verse, the solo. The music was . . . well, a bit weird. The band was playing. But it was not playing *together* . . .

Ooer. Time for the solo. Eric went three feet in the air and landed on the big red pedal . . .

"Two, three, *four*," said Buddy in the Big Cab.

As Eric's pick came down on the strings, he noticed a strange thing. All of a sudden, the music got deeper and darker and thicker. Eric's mind flew away from imaginary birds and back into his fingers. And the groove came together, *thunk*.

Eric did very little thinking at the best of times, and none at all while he was playing solos. If he had, he would have thought that it was as if there were a couple of extra people in the band.

Colin de Weasel sat in his office and polished his dark glasses. His eyes were pink and shifty, with a tendency to water. Through the little window that looked out onto the auditorium came the sound of Death Eric. Colin de Weasel's lip took on a nasty curl. He despised people who would spend fifteen quid to get into his club. And he thought the people who played the garbage they came to listen to needed their heads examined. Colin de Weasel hated music almost as much as he loved money.

Ho, ho, thought Colin de Weasel, stuffing the bulging suitcase into a backpack. Off I go.

It was hot in the Big Cab.

"OK," said Eric, on the stage. "Last tune." Feedback. "'S gonna be—"

"Got to be 'Pig Train,'" said Lou. "Surely."

"That's what it says on the set list," said Buddy, peering at his screen.

"'Donkey!'" said Eric.

"Oh dear," said Lou. "Poor Dad. Bottled out."

"Wait," said Buddy, watching the CCTV screen above the keyboard.

The door from de Weasel's office had opened. A head with a beard and a mustache appeared around the door. It looked left and right. Then it crept out into the auditorium. On its stooped back was a backpack, with sleeping bag and bedroll.

Buddy hesitated a moment. On stage, the band thundered on, playing pretty well now, encouraged by the secret assistance from the Big Cab. Then he thumbed the TALK button of his walkie-talkie.

The man with the beard and the mustache and the backpack was three steps out of his door when a big hand closed on his left arm. He was three and one-eighth steps out of the door and struggling when another big hand closed on his right arm. Then he was taking a lot of steps, but none of them made any difference, because his feet were ten inches off the ground, and the large roadie on his left and the large roadie on his right were giving him a swift bum's rush toward the stage door.

"They'll be fine on their own," said Lou, putting down her guitar.

"*Much* improved," said Buddy, switching off his keyboard.

Inserting earplugs, the children let themselves out of the Big Cab and into the roar of a Death Eric final number with an audience going mental. They went up the stairs, into the dressing room. Enid was already there, sprawled huge but elegant in an armchair. Buddy poured apple juice for himself and his sister. Then they sat down and composed their features.

The door opened. Two roadies came in. Between them was a small bearded man. Actually, a not-very-small bearded man; it was just that the roadies were exceptionally big.

"Put him down," said Buddy.

"Pull his hair," said Lou.

"Er . . . ," said the left-hand roadie, a nicely brought-up giant who thought pulling hair was girly.

The right-hand roadie was a girl, so she had no problem with hair pulling. She pulled. "Yuk!" she cried. "A wig!"

"Now the beard," said Lou.

The left-hand roadie was getting the idea. He yanked the beard. It came away.

Colin de Weasel stood scowling, crew-cut, and clean-shaven between the giants.

"*Nice* one," said Enid admiringly.

"The backpack," said Buddy, gimlet-eyed. "Open up, please."

"I'm going camping," said de Weasel. "It's just some old clothes, tinsa beans, you know."

"No," said Lou, smiling sweetly. "But we'd love to look. It would be so educational."

"She'd love to look," said the roadie, removing de Weasel's arm from the backpack strap.

"It's private," said de Weasel plaintively.

"Tell me," said Buddy, as the other roadie disentangled the other arm. "How many people came through the door this evening?"

"Oh, about two hundred," said de Weasel. "Something like that, anyway."

"Ah," said Buddy. "I made it a bit more than that. Roadies?"

"We counted," said the girl roadie. "Two thousand four hundred and twelve."

"That's what I meant," said de Weasel, blushing.

The other roadie pulled a suitcase out of the backpack.

"Open it," said Buddy, remorseless. "Search him."

"It's private," said de Weasel. "Ooer." For he was being thoroughly searched by the girl roadie, while the other one popped the catches on the suitcase and opened the lid.

"Funny camping gear," said Lou.

The suitcase was full to the top with ten-squid notes.

"Nice *one*," said Enid.

"So," said Buddy, finishing his examination of the wad of papers the roadie had taken from the promoter's pockets and giving it back to him. "The entrance money, I do believe. And you were going to go on a camping holiday with ... well, thirty-six thousand-odd squids, am I right?"

"Heh, heh, very droll," said the bloke roadie.

Lou was riffling through the top layer of bank notes. "Well, then," she said. "That's that."

"Caught him bang to rights," said the girl roadie.

"Red-handed," said the bloke roadie.

"With his fingers in the till."

Buddy said, "It is not illegal to carry money."

"Wha?"

"For instance," said Buddy, "I bet you've got some in your pocket."

"Eighteen pounds," said the roadie. "Beer money."

"Well, Mr. de Weasel is probably carrying champagne money. There is no law against it."

"But—," said Lou.

"No buts. Mr. de Weasel is going about his lawful business. Sorry you were troubled, Mr. de Weasel. On your way!"

Colin de Weasel looked right. He looked left. He could not believe his luck in either direction. He picked up the suitcase and slid like a rat out of the door.

8

There was a moment's frozen silence in the room, unless you counted Death Eric's hurricane of feedback and 2,412 punters screaming for more. Then Lou said, "What did you do *that* for?"

"Follow him," said Buddy to the girl roadie. "And don't be seen."

"I'll go," said Enid.

"You'll be recognized."

"No way." Enid left the dressing room.

"Buddy!" cried Lou, horrified. "Will you tell me

why you have just let that thief run away with the door money so we will have nothing to buy clothes and all that? What are you *doing*?"

"Look at this," said Buddy. "It was in his pocket." He held out a piece of paper.

It was a letter. *Dear Colin,* it said. *I see the lads are playing at yours. Bring me all the gate money or my bodyguard will break your legs. Yours affectionately Per Spire p.p. Doom Management.*

Enid came back in. She had changed into a chic leather jacket, designer jeans, and high-heeled boots. Her face was exquisitely made up, her hair caught at the nape of her neck in a charming chignon.

"Wow!" said Buddy.

"You look like a million dollars!" said Lou.

"Several million, I hope," said Enid. "Now point me at 'em."

Buddy and Lou watched her sashay into the night, huge and beautiful. The Wheel and Martyr crouched among the puddles of its car park, pulsating with another encore. A dog loped, howling, into the night. "She will follow Colin," said Buddy. "He will lead us to Per. He will suspect nothing."

"You're so clever!" said Lou.

"Life is not all fairy tales," said Buddy irritatingly.

Ten minutes later, the telephone rang.

"Yeah?" said Buddy.

A voice came through the phone. It was like Enid's voice, but higher and more girly. It giggled.

"Well?" said Buddy.

"It's just that—ooooh!—Colin and me are in Colin's sports car, he's got a Lamborari you know, and he asked me for a ride because he said I am really pretty. Anyway, he is taking me to this house on Wahoo Beach and we are going to live happily ever after." There was the noise of a giggle and a slap. "Oo, you are awful," she said, apparently to de Weasel. Then the battery ran out.

"Wha?" said Lou.

"Hmm," said Buddy. "Where's Wahoo Beach?"

"Thirty miles out of town."

"Let's go there."

"It is the longest beach in the country," said Lou. "Forty miles long. What is Enid *doing*?"

"Telling us where she is," said Buddy. "Roughly. A bit too roughly for my liking."

"So we've lost her, poor Enid. And Colin de awful Weasel," said Lou. "And his suitcase."

"Our suitcase," said Buddy.

Suddenly, the car park was full of people. The

gig was over. From the happy expressions and the clicking of lighters, it seemed that Death Eric had played a blinder.

For free.

"You didn't play 'Pig Train,'" said Lou to her father over a Chinese takeaway.

"Nevermore," said Eric.

"But people love it," said Lou.

Eric ate three forkfuls of rice, spilling most of it. "When they say 'spare ribs,'" he said, "do they mean like car spares?"

"No," said Lou. "Why won't you play 'Pig Train'?"

"Because the bird looked at me."

"So you'll never play it again?"

"Not," said Eric, "until the bird comes up to me and says, like, 'Death Eric, you are playing just lovely. The curse is lifted. God Save the Queen.'"

"As simple as that?" said Lou, feeling the blood rather drain from her head.

"Yeah."

"Fine."

Obviously it was time for bed.

*

There was no news of Enid in the night. The next morning, the morning of the Dark Holler gig, dawned fine and clear. The band watched it happen, then went to bed. Naturally, Buddy and Lou were fast asleep. They rose early, at about lunchtime.

"School in a week," said Lou.

"Can't wait," said Buddy. "Any more cereal?"

"Last packet," said Lou.

There was a grim, silent pause. Then Lou said, "I tried on last term's uniform last night. It's too small. *Much* too small."

"I tried next term's syllabus with last term's scientific instruments," said Buddy. "It can't be done."

More silence, broken only by the sound of cereal being eaten. Buddy finished his bowl and reached out his hand for the packet.

Lou said, "It's empty."

"Oh."

"There's toast. Well, a bit of toast. Not much butter. No jam."

"No, thanks."

More silence.

The telephone rang. Buddy picked it up.

"Hello?" said a voice. A girl's voice. A girl's voice with tears in it.

"Ugh," said Buddy, and handed the phone to his sister.

"Hello?" said Lou.

An odd noise was coming out of the earpiece. It sounded as if someone had left a tap running.

"Hello?" said Lou again.

A voice was saying, "Mump." Or sobbing. Probably sobbing.

"It's not as bad as all that," said Lou, taking a guess.

"It is," said the voice. "It *is*!"

"Enid?"

"Mump."

"Enid?" said Lou. She had never heard Enid this upset about anything before. It was deeply shocking. "Why don't you tell me about it?" More waterworks. "Well?" said Lou. "What happened?"

"He saw me watching him and he stopped the car and he said, 'Hop in, big girl, love the jacket,' and I thought, this is the best way to follow someone."

"Oh yeah," said Lou, who couldn't help thinking that Enid was extremely foolish for a grown-up, even though she absolutely did understand about the clothes. "So what happened then?"

"He took me out into the middle of nowhere,"

said the roadie. "He stopped the car in a forest type sort of place. He told me to get out. He said I was a spy! I don't know how he guessed."

"Well, you are quite . . . distinctive," said Lou.

"Did you cover up your PROPERTY OF DEATH ERIC tattoo?" said Buddy.

"Anyone can forget," said Enid. "It is an emotional time."

"Yep," said Lou. "Poor Enid. So you are upset because you are in a forest and you need collecting and maybe breakfast, so we'll come and get you and then you won't be so upset anymore."

"I'm not upset because I'm in a forest because I am not in a forest," said Enid. "I'm in Wahoo Beach."

"Wha?" said Lou. "How?"

"You don' think I am goin' to let a two-timing hornswoggling poodlefaking chauvinist thieving ironed-jeans creep like that get away with what he was trying to get away with, do you?" said Enid. "I flagged down a car. I said, 'Follow that Lamborari!' and the geezer in the car, well, truck actually, said, 'No way.' So I tied him to a tree and pinched the truck and followed the creep myself. I was in a bad mood. It's wearing jeans. You can't get the nicotine patches onto your legs. And now I am outside the house where the creep is."

"In a stolen truck?" said Lou.

Enid sniffed. "'Course not," she said. "I left it outside an old-people's home and walked the last bit."

"That's all right, then," said Lou. Even in her present emotional turmoil, Enid was a genius. "So what now?"

"I'm going to watch Per."

"Per?"

"Who else?" *Sniff.*

"Whaddayamean, watch him?"

"Colin de Weasel took the suitcase to Per's house," said Enid. "I can see him now. He's just taken the suitcase into his garage."

There was silence. Even in the midst of her sympathy for Enid, Lou looked at her brother with total respect. His plan had worked like a dream.

"So it's really true about Per?" said Lou.

"Of course it is." *Sniff.*

"But you . . . loved him," said Lou.

"Mmm," said Enid, blowing her nose in a manner that sounded totally final. "Brilliant. What they call an evil genius, I suppose. He has shown himself to be a thieving yellow-bellied herring-gutted lily-livered son of a boar. Plus there is another girl with him. So now my love has turned to hate and the scales have fallen from my eyes and I am going to go right down there and fill them in."

"Hold on," said Buddy. "He'll have you arrested."

"For our sakes," said Lou. "Please wait."

"Oh, all right," said Enid.

"What's the address?"

"He's at 666 Wahoo Beach, Massive Studios. It's the one with the bodyguards and the electrified security fence and the remote-control gates. I'm coming back now. We have plans to make." The phone went down.

"Well," said Lou. "She got over that broken heart quite quickly."

Buddy looked at his watch. He said, "It's one o'clock. And the band is playing at eight, right?"

"So we go and sort out Per. And then we come back and listen to the band and climb into the Big Cab if necessary."

"It's a long way to Wahoo Beach. There's a security fence, remote-control gates. Is Per going to just, like, hand the money over?"

"No," said Buddy, frowning.

"It all calls to mind," said Lou, "'The Tale of the Puppet Show, the Witch, and the Children.'" Her fingers went to the pocket in her blazer and she drew out the book. "'Once upon a—'"

"No *way*," said Buddy. "I have a plan—"

"The story," said Lou firmly, "is about a wicked witch who stole a magic duck from some children. Luckily she stopped to watch a puppet show on her way home. So the children's father was able to sneak up behind her, bop her over the head, and nick back the duck."

"If you think Eric is going to bop anyone, you—"

"You are missing the point," said Lou.

The children went to work, issuing orders and assembling equipment. Shortly after two, Enid returned, sat down, and drank a cup of tea. Her gigantic face bore the traces of the night's strong emotions, but she looked calm and resolute.

"Easy," she said when Lou had explained the plan. "Can do. D'you think it'll work?"

"It's got to," said Lou.

"What about the band? If you don't get to the stadium in time to help out?"

"We have ways of improving their confidence," said Lou.

"Good. Because if they mess up the Dark Holler,

they're . . . well."

Buddy and Lou nodded. If you messed up the Dark Holler, the crowd would tear you limb from limb.

If you were lucky.

The surf was booming on Wahoo Beach. A couple of muscle-bound oafs were doing push-ups for the benefit of their girlfriends, who were smiling politely and thinking about something else. Out on the sea side of where the waves were breaking, Buddy and Lou were sitting on surfboards.

"I can't actually surf," said Buddy. He was wearing board shorts, which were not at all his style. He felt wrongly dressed and deeply unhappy.

"Just as well," said Lou. Lou was actually not a bad surfer. She was dressed in a neat black one-piece bathing suit by Gucci, and she felt perfectly at home—rather excited, even. "It's going to have to be realistic." Her waterproof wrist radio beeped. She put it to her ear. "In position," she said.

"Gulp," said Buddy.

Lou was looking over her shoulder, so he looked too, and wished he hadn't.

A hill of water was rolling in from the horizon.

It seemed to be a largish hill and it was getting steeper.

"Placing the hands in the water, *paddle*," said Lou, paddling.

Buddy paddled too. The hill of water swooshed up behind him. It seemed to be making a roaring noise, but there was no time to look around.

"We're off!" cried Lou.

The slope of water rolled under the boards, getting steeper, until it was more like a cliff than a hill. Buddy realized that his board was shooting toward the shore. It was a lovely feeling, like flying, really. He got up on his knees. "Wheee!" he cried, admiring his sister, who was standing on her board, knees bent, arms out, carving a white V of spray from the face of the wave.

Buddy decided that he would stand up too. He hopped to his feet. For a split second everything was perfect. Then everything was the opposite.

The top of the wave, which had been green and smooth, turned suddenly white and toppling. For another split second, Buddy stood high on the wave, saying, "Ooer." Then the crest flicked forward and hurled him into the trough. He hit the water. The wave broke. The world turned soaking wet and noisier than Death Eric playing "Doom Doom" and he knew what it must feel like to be a small pair of underpants in a gigantic washing machine. And the last clear thought he had was: *This is what was meant to happen.*

From her safer bit of the wave, the more skillful Lou watched with pride as her brave brother was swooshed off his board and smacked into the spume. Then she pulled out, dived neatly in, and started to look for him.

Grungus Fist watched from the terrace of 666 Wahoo Beach Massive Studios. "Hur," he said, larding sun oil into the hair on his back. "Wipeout. Bad one."

"Oh, *stop* it," said Per Spire, by his side. "How I hate *people*."

"Me too," said the curvy lady on the lounger at his side.

"Nobody's interested in you, Desirée," said Per.

Desirée pouted. Then she thought that while her lips were stuck out, she might as well put some more lipstick on them. No effort wasted that way. Actually, she was kinda sick of sitting on this terrace with Per and his bodyguard. Per was OK in a rich, slimy way, but Grungus was not OK in any way known to man or woman—

"Maybe he drowned," said Grungus, licking his scarred lips.

"Nah," said Per, more for the pleasure of disagreeing than because he was interested.

Down by the edge of the sea, a child in a one-piece black bathing suit was dragging a child in board shorts up the beach by one leg. The child being dragged was either alive or dead. It made no difference to Per. Reaching for his calculator, he started adding up his money. Per was a good adder, and the total worked out the same every time. But somehow he never got tired of doing it.

The beach was not too wide, which was just as well, because dragging even a medium-sized brother through dry sand by one foot is hard work, particularly when the brother is complaining in a quiet but severe voice.

"The sand is going up my shorts," said Buddy.

"Shh," said Lou. "Not long now."

Massive Studios at 666 Wahoo Beach was not really a studio at all. It was a very smart collection of glass boxes with a Spanish tiled roof. The terrace, planted on legs over the beach, carried a load of chic driftwood sculptures of whales, and three people. Lou thought that one of them looked dangerous but stupid (she meant Grungus). She knew the other one was dangerous, clever, and a treacherous thieving creep (she meant Per, lying there with his gray hair and his gray skin, with his gray silk swimming trunks). She did not know if the third one was dangerous, but she did not look it. She did not look very clever either, but then it is not easy to look clever when you are sticking your lips out like a duck's beak so you can lash on the lipstick. Lou was encouraged by the resemblance to a duck. It reminded her of the Brothers Grime. She decided that it was to the duck lady that she should address herself. She checked her watch. It said one minute to four. She squeezed Buddy's heel.

"Oooh," groaned Buddy.

"Ahem," said Lou. "I think my little brother might be drowned."

"Nah," said Grungus. "'E moaned."

The duck lady was on her feet. "Poor *thing*!" she said. "How *awful*! Bring him up here quickly!"

"He's sandy," said Per, not looking up from his

calculator, which was still showing the same lovely result.

"If I could just use your mobile to call an ambulance?" said Lou.

"Of *course!*" cried the duck lady.

"Ahem," said Lou, taking the teeny phone. "Nine . . . one . . . er . . ."

"One," said the duck lady. "Allow me to introduce myself. I am Desirée. Can I give him mouth-to-mouth?"

"Hak," said Buddy hastily. "Oo me chest infection. Koff."

"I think he's coming around," said Desirée.

"He could be concussed," said Lou, checking her watch again. The minute hand said four o'clock.

Surprisingly prompt ambulance sirens sounded on the inland side of the house.

"Er . . . ," said Grungus.

"Let 'em in," sighed Per, starting his calculations again.

"Er . . . ," said Grungus.

"Don't say er!" shrieked kind Desirée. "Open the gates."

Grungus sighed. He pressed the button of the remote gate control.

"*Thank* you!" cried Lou, seizing his hand and slobbering on it gratefully.

"Oi!" cried Grungus, for Lou had somehow managed to knock the remote-control gate opener from his hand and was now burrowing in the sand at the foot of the balcony, apparently looking for it but actually burying it deeper with every hectic scrabble.

"So much noise," said Per Spire. "Now look what you made me do, I have to start over!" He pressed CANCEL on his calculator, moved his chair away, and started totting up again. There seemed to be more than one ambulance siren.

Not his problem.

Grungus went to meet the ambulances. He did not hold with visitors. Grungus was highly security conscious. As far as he was concerned, kids who drowned had only themselves to blame, and Desirée might be pretty, but she was a chink in Mr. Spire's armor. Grungus trotted down the steps and into the gravel patch at the back of the house. The security gates were open, of course. There seemed to be three ambulances. Grungus thought this was too many for one kid, but hey, if they wanted to waste good money, that was their problem.

He frowned. They were funny-looking ambulances. Two of them looked like Transit vans with insulating-tape red crosses stuck on the side. The third looked like . . . well, a bulldozer, with an insulating-tape red cross on the blade.

Grungus frowned. He groped in his small mind for medical uses of the bulldozer. He did not find any. The bulldozer turned toward the garage. The driver did not look like an ambulance driver. He had long hair and tattoos and ragged jeans and rigger's boots. Actually he looked more . . .

like . . .

a . . .

roadie.

Somewhere in Grungus's skull, a penny dropped. He opened his mouth to roar. But at that moment a cargo net fell over him and he found himself hoisted into the sky. He caught a brief glimpse of a crane. Then he was upside down and a couple of roadies were attaching the net to an electricity pole.

He grunted. He struggled. But, in the end, all he could do was watch as the bulldozer lined up, spewed black smoke from its stack, and drove its blade into the side of the garage.

*

On the beach in front of the terrace, there was plenty of noise. Desirée was stroking Buddy's hair and talking in a high, excited voice about miracles. Buddy was saying honestly he just fell off his surfboard and if she tried mouth-to-mouth he would sue. Lou was saying thank you very much it was time they were going. And Per was saying shut up, he was trying to concentrate, and anyway this was private property.

"Ohh!" cried Desirée. "So *cruel*!"

"Tell them I'll be calling the police," said Per.

There was a crash from the other side of the house, followed by the sound of a roof falling in.

"Wha?" said Per, surprised for perhaps the first time in his life.

"It sounds to me," said Lou, "as if someone has just driven a bulldozer into your garage."

"Really?" said Per, going back to the calculator. Then his finger felt above the buttons. *"Wha?"* He stared at Lou. He frowned. "Don't I know you from somewhere?"

"Our house, maybe. You practically lived in it for about twenty years."

Per's gray face went white. "Omigod," he said.

"And you get ten percent of what the band gets."

Per nodded, or perhaps he was shaking with fear.

"So we are going to take away your property."

"All of it?"

"Except the tools and the lawn mowers and all that."

"What we want," said Buddy, "is the money."

"But it's not yours," said Per.

"Oh yes it is," said Buddy. "Listen."

There were grinding noises and shouts of delight and the sound of roadies passing suitcases from hand to hand.

"Yeah," said Per. "Waitaminute. All right. I was, like, looking after it for you. For the band." He smiled. It looked like a corpse grinning. He used the grin to bite a nail. "I heard . . . things weren't going well."

"Because you weren't around to help," said Lou.

Per's mouth went down at the corners. "And you wanna know why?" he said. "Because that band is all washed up, is why. Do the guys play like they used to?" Per's cold gray eyes looked from one child to the other, grew more confident. "Oh no," he said. "Oooooh no. It was only when I fixed things up for them that they could function. I worked my fingers to the bone. For a measly . . . ten . . . percent."

"They're doing fine," said Lou.

"Oh yeah? And they're playing the Dark Holler tonight. And the crowd will want them to play 'Pig Train.' And Eric won't, will he? Because a bird told him not to. And the crowd will tear them apart." He paused. "If they're lucky."

"Thief," said Buddy.

"Ha!" said Per. "Take it all. There's more where that came from."

"We'll have that, too," said Lou. "We'll take what's in the garage—"

"—and in the house," said Buddy.

"—and all the contracts. And we'll do the accounts, and you can have what's yours, and it will be plenty."

"All the money in the world," said Per nastily, "will not make Death Eric into anything but a bunch of losers. They've lost their bottle."

"That's as may be," said Lou. But Per was clever enough to put his finger right on the sore spot. She had an awful feeling he might be right.

"Watch your lip," said Buddy. But for him, too, the manager's words rang true.

226

"Well," said Desirée, "*I* think Death Eric is *fabulous*. Can I come to the gig with you?"

"But—," said Per. It was no use. His silky spell was broken and he knew it.

"Beautiful lady," said Buddy, with a low, courtly bow, "you are more than welcome."

And they walked through the house to the vans, scooping up some wads of money on the way. The money was not important. Desirée had said a very nice thing and they were wrapped in a warm, lovely glow.

Confidence. That was all you needed.

"Done it," said Enid, handing out towels and dry clothes.

The children introduced Desirée, who looked very excited to be with roadies.

Enid said, scowling, "You're Per's girlfriend."

"Not anymore," said Desirée. "The guy's a cockroach."

"Correct," said Enid. She reached for a nicotine patch, then changed her mind and beamed at Desirée instead. "On we go, eh, sister?"

"On we go, sister," said Desirée.

"OK," said Enid. "The reserve crew's looking

after the band. It's going fine. Lads are in great spirits, apparently. We go to the bank, right?"

"Right."

From his cargo net high on the electricity pole, Grungus watched the convoy of vans roll through the security fence and into the dunes, heading for the distant fumes and skyscrapers of Smoke City. Someone cut the rope holding up the net. He fell to earth, knocking a fair-sized dent in a rock. Looking up through the meshes, he saw Per Spire standing over him. Disentangling himself, he struggled to his feet.

"Get after them," said Per. "I want it back."

"Gimme my wages," said Grungus.

"Er . . . ," said Per, biting a nail. "They've taken all the money. Just at the moment . . . that is, if you could wait a week, while I—"

"Sorry," said Grungus. "No pay, no work."

"But—"

Grungus turned away. He began to walk up into the dunes, heading for the distant towers of Smoke City. He had no job and his ex-boss was a creep. But Death Eric was playing the Dark Holler in something under four hours, and Death Eric was the greatest rock-and-roll band in the world. Back on the road and, according to rumor, playing real well.

Be there or be square, said Grungus Fist to himself.

Actually, that was what most of Smoke City was saying to itself.

Smoke City, population one million.

"Can't we go any faster?" said Lou.

"It's the traffic," said Enid, who was driving.

The traffic was indeed thick as mud. They had dropped off the money at a branch of the bank, where it had taken twenty people an hour to count it, using automatic machines. Now they were back in the vans, heading for the deeply unfashionable part of the Smoke that was home to the Dark Holler.

"Short cuts?" said Buddy.

"Tried 'em," said Enid grimly.

"Shorter cuts?"

"OK," said Enid, turning sharp left through the plate-glass window of a butcher's shop, crashing through the back wall, emerging in an ice-cream parlor, removing the counter, bursting the plate-glass window out into the street, and taking her place in the traffic jam on the far side. She turned to Buddy. "See what I mean?" she said.

"Not good."

Lou looked up from her book. She said, "An hour from now the band is going to hit the stage, and Dad will be thinking about the bird curse and Fingers is going to be covered in mower oil and Kenyatta is going to be dreaming of fish, and . . . well."

Enid rolled down the window and removed a string of sausages from the rearview mirror. "Where you goin'?" she said to the driver of the next car.

"Death Eric concert."

"Me too," said the driver of the next car, which had eight passengers.

"Me too," said everyone in the road, until they sounded like an army of owls.

Lou took out her phone and dialed.

"Who you ringing?" said Buddy.

"**SELFRODS**. It's open late tonight."

"Ah," said Buddy. Lou was a keen shopper and it might take her mind off things.

"Hello?" said Lou into the telephone. "**SELFRODS**? Gimme the Zoo. Zoo? Can I speak with your Superintendent of Talking Ravens? Thanks."

There was a pause. Then she said, "Super-intendent? How do you do? Lou Thrashmettle here. Yes, he's my dad. Are you? So's everyone else. Listen, I need a raven, one that talks. Large size. To be delivered to Death Eric on the stage at the Dark Holler just before the first number. Gift card? No. But you've got to teach it to say something." She explained. "Got it? Good. Put it on the account. We are back in credit."

The van lurched forward.

The van stopped.

Buddy gazed out of the window, deep in thought.

Lou read her book.

So the long day wore on.

And the long evening.

Pretty soon, they were close enough to the Dark Holler to hear the sound check. Then they could hear the warm-up band. Then the roar of the crowd.

"Only two miles to go," said Enid.

The band would be on any minute. There was a horrible silence in the van now.

"If only Per was here," said a roadie. "He'd know what to do. Oi! Yaroo! Stoppit!"

"But," said Enid, when the punishment was over, "we could ask ourselves, what would Per have *done*?"

"Called in a chopper," said Buddy.

"Genius," said Lou, closing her book.

Enid was already dialing.

The traffic moved forward a foot and a half. A couple of roadies crawled onto the van roof and put an enormous black insulating-tape H on the white metal surface. Through the open windows, the sound of the Dark Holler was a steady roar. Above the roar came a familiar noise: the sound of motorbikes revving and cows mooing, hugely amplified. And behind it, the sound of a guitar feeding back; a big, hefty guitar, with plenty of roar and more than a hint of screech.

There was the sound of a huge crowd going mad. Then the van windows bulged inward to the sound of a power chord. It became a riff. Bass and drums came in. And away went Death Eric into "Chainsaw."

Lou looked around her at the other drivers in the traffic jam. Heads were already nodding. Five bars in, heads were banging. And that included several policemen and a busload of nuns.

"Sounds like he got the raven," she said.

"A highly confident performance," said Buddy.

"Probably won't last," said Sid the Soothsayer.

"Sid, I think I may love you," cried Enid, embracing him.

"Oh! Look! Over there!" cried Lou. "Good old **SELFRODS**!"

And there, stuck in the traffic a hundred feet away, was a burgundy-red van with the word **SELFRODS** written in gold under a gold coat of arms.

"Won't be a minute!" cried Lou, leaping out of the window.

Boom, boom, boom, went her feet on the roofs of the jammed cars. *Boom, boom, boom* went the distant but still extremely loud bass guitar of Fingers Trubshaw. And bang, bang, bang went the heads of the oblivious drivers in the traffic jam that had just become a drive-in rock concert.

By the middle eight of "Chainsaw," Lou was standing on the running board of the **SELFRODS** van. "Hey!" she cried. "Stop headbanging!"

The driver stopped. He put on his burgundy uniform cap and turned to her with a dazed look.

"I just wanted to say," said Lou, "that I think **SELFRODS** is the greatest shop in the world."

"Oh, I dunno," said the driver, going pink.

"I mean you always get through. Even at short notice. It's amazing."

"Nah," said the driver, shaking a regretful head. "Not tonight. I mean, look at this traffic. I got some stuff for those geezers playing in there. But can I get through? No way, José."

"Stuff?" said Lou, suddenly pale. "Like . . . a bird?"

"Educated crow or somefink, I dunno. It's been swearing something cruel."

"Bleep," said a harsh, croaking voice from the van's cargo hold.

Lou reeled. "Raven," she said.

"Doesn't sound too sane to me," said the driver.

"But . . . Eric's *playing*."

"'Course he is," said the driver. "That's what he does. He knows he's good at it. And so do we."

Lou said, "Give me that bird."

"Wha?"

Hastily, Lou explained. By the time she had finished and the driver had handed her the cage, the air was full of nattering helicopter rotors. *Boom boom boom*, went her feet on the car roofs. *Doom doom doom*, went the bass of Fingers Trubshaw. *Wokka wokka wokka*, went the Sea King chopper as it floated down from the sky and hovered over the van's roof.

In they got. Off they took. Up they went, until the Dark Holler was a doughnut far below and Death

Eric's lasers pinged around them in a rainbow. Down they went, into the backstage area. Out they jumped and up to the stage door they ran.

"Look out, raven," said Lou to the cage in her hand. "It's going to be noisy."

"Birds don't understand," said Buddy.

"This one does," said the raven, surprisingly.

Into the door they went. The noise hit them.

Part of it was Death Eric, and to say that Death Eric was steaming is like saying that Niagara Falls is water dripping off a rock. The other part of it was the audience, and to say the audience was roaring is like saying that a hurricane is a slight movement of air.

"This is going to be rubbish," said Sid the Soothsayer, then, "Gerroff!" as everyone hugged him.

They went to stand at the side of the stage. The number had ended. Eric shifted a couple of snakes away from his face and wandered toward the mike stand. Along the front of the stage a forest of arms waved like sea anemones.

"Next tune," he mumbled. "You may have heard it before. Wassit called? Er . . . dunno." He grinned the legendary Eric Thrashmettle grin. "Two, *three*," he said. Then he jumped seven feet in the air and came down bang on the big pedal, and the first chord went howling out across the city like an intercontinental ballistic banshee. And Death Eric was thundering again, and the crowd went mad.

Lou looked at Buddy. Buddy looked at Lou. "'Pig Train,'" they said, or rather mouthed, because obviously nobody for miles could hear himself think, unless he could lip-read in a mirror. "Dad and the lads have Got It Back."

Lou put down the cage containing the now-unnecessary raven. She opened the door. The raven waddled out onto the stage, cocked its head to one side, spread its wings, and launched itself into the air.

OUTRO

The raven glided up, past the lights and into the darkness. It was a raven that valued its freedom, but it did not set off straight away for the tall timber. High above the stadium, it wheeled on stiffened wings. Below it, the Dark Holler stage looked like the glint in a massive eyeball. From it there came the tramp of a heartbeat slowing and a moan like an animal in pain. Slowing heartbeats are of great interest to ravens. They are part of the food situation.

But this raven had had a large tea, so food was

not uppermost in its thoughts, such as they were. There were other things on its not very big mind: things for which it had been trained, but which it also wanted to do, out of sheer niceness. It tilted a few feathers against the air. It began a long, sweeping glide back toward the stage.

On the stage, the band was nearly at the end of Part One of "Pig Train." They were slowing it down, right down until it stopped, ready to crash back in again with Part Two, brisk and cheery as an air strike on a tank regiment.

The rhythm section ground to a halt. Eric's guitar sobbed and howled. The sound tumbled into the night and died away. A million people held their breath, fumbling in their anoraks for lighters.

With a dry rustle of feathers, the raven swooped out of the darkness and stood, blinking, on the microphone. It said, "Death Eric, you are playing just lovely. The curse is lifted. God Save the Queen."

"Ta, mate," said Eric absentmindedly. "Glad you like it. 'Scuse me, here comes Part Two. A-THREE, fah." Into the air he jumped, and down on the big pedal he came, and away howled Death Eric into the ozone, and off flapped the raven to its homeland of stone circles and small, rocky hills.

In the wings, Lou and Buddy shook hands. It looked as if it would be an excellent autumn term, warm with cashmere and filled with hard sums easily doable thanks to the splendid scientific instruments available at **SELFRODS**.

"It definitely won't last," lip-wrote Sid the Soothsayer.

Everyone patted him on the back. When someone like him said something like that, you could be one hundred percent sure that people were going to live happily ever after.

ACKNOWLEDGMENTS

I am very grateful to F. Jones of Wrexham, Fish Fryers' Sundriesmen, for their invaluable advice on technical matters. And, of course, to the many geniuses, lunatics, and reprobates I met in my travels through the world of rock and roll. Since I can remember few of their names, they had better all remain anonymous. Many of them prefer it that way. Except the stars, that is. And they know who they are. Or did once.

S.Ll.

DEATH ERIC:
BATS, RATS, 'N' CHEESE

Lifelong fan and serious rock journalist Slick Fortescue-Watson-Fford meets rock gods DEATH ERIC.

There is a bat crawling along the floor of the corridor outside the dressing room. I stoop to caress it. "Nice," says a voice. I look up, and my heart skips a beat.

I am in the presence of a Legend.

"In," says the voice behind the hair. Eric Thrashmettle's hair.

I go into the dressing room. Are my jeans right? Are my trainers worthy? The door closes. There is a smell of feet and frying. I sink gratefully into a chair. Death Eric are all around me.

I am hanging out with a Legend.

I consult my notes. I try to think up a really clever question. No luck. Forty-three minutes pass.

"I want to ask you five really stupid questions," I say, in the end.

"Thank goodness," say the band members, in close harmony.

Here they are.

1. What's your fave animal?
Eric: Ummmm . . .
Fingers: I had a bear once. Called Davies. And I have a sheep called Mildred now. She is useful for nibbling lawns short and she has come to look on me as a friend.
Kenyatta: Mostly I am into fish.
Eric: . . . bats. Many, many bats.

2. What's your fave food?
Eric: Errr . . .
Fingers: Lunch. Some fool once said I liked jelly babies. People started to throw them. Jelly babies hurt when flung.

Kenyatta: Calm down there, Trubshaw. Fried stuff is the wave of the future, you mark my words.

Eric: . . . oats. And cheese, if you don't have to make it. And bats. Many, many bats.

3. Hair or no hair?

Eric: Umm . . .

Fingers: Hair? Love it. The lawn of the head, I always say. Pay attention to it and life will take on a deeper, richer meaning.

Kenyatta: A person can pay too much attention to hair. But you got to say this for it, it makes a great thing to put a hat on.

Eric: . . . difficult. You got to paint it green sometimes. Or dye it. Or it becomes home to bats. Many, many bats.

4. What is your hope for the future of Planet Earth?

Eric: Ummm . . .

Fingers: That its lawns may be smooth and green, and that there should be tolerance for all living things as long as they are vegetables.

Kenyatta: Yeah, like what Trubshaw said, except not just vegetables.

Eric: . . . yeah, lawns, vegetables, living things, many bats obviously. Can we go soon?

5. Just one more question. Step with me, if you will, onto the Dark Side. What is your greatest fear?

Eric: (quick as a striking mamba) Nervous ravens overhead . . .

Fingers: A long lawn and a blunt mower.

Kenyatta: Not finding Alphonse Quing the Sanitary Man and force-feeding him fried rat.

Eric: . . . and not being able to play music.

Fingers: Yeah.

Kenyatta: Yeah.

Thanks, Death Eric. Pig TRAIIIIIIIIIIIIIIIINNNN!

GLOSSARY

Anorak: Smelly, damp, dark green, food-stained, semi-water-proof coat worn by festival-goers immune to fashion.

Artics: Semi-trailer trucks.

Bang to rights: There is no translation for this, since it means something between "red-handed" and "over a barrel."

Bass bins: Large bass speakers that give rise to earthquakelike effects in front of the stage.

Bat scratchings: Pork scratchings are deep-fried pork rinds, so no prizes for guessing what bat scratchings are.

Black pudding: I can scarcely bring myself to describe the stuff that goes into this most British of breakfast dishes. Oh, all right then. Blood and fat in a sausage skin, fried till sticky. Yum.

Blinder: Something really totally radically blindingly excellent.

Bonnet: In the U.S., cars have a hood in front and a trunk in back. In Britain, they have a bonnet in front and a boot in back.

Bread-and-butter pudding: A British pudding made of bread and butter, much loved by simple folk like rock stars. Oh, and it has raisins in it. Sometimes.

Breakdown truck: Tow truck.

Brickbat: A rock. Maybe half a housebrick. Or maybe a whole one.

Budgie: Budgerigar, a singing cage bird beloved by all Britons.

Cabinet Minister: Presidential adviser, British style.

Car park: Parking lot.

CCTV: Closed Circuit TV.

Chips: What you guys call fries.

Crisps: Potato chips.

Dusted: She knocked the dust off him, didn't she? Because he had been on the floor, hadn't he?

Fags: Cigarettes.

Fifty-pound notes: Currency bills, to the value of fifty squids (see below).

Giving it the verbal: Talking too much.

Her Maj: Short for "Her Majesty Queen Elizabeth the Second of Great Britain and Northern Ireland, Defender of the Faith . . ." and so on.

HP Sauce: A brown mixture of vinegar and rare spices with which roadies slather their snacks. Highly corrosive.

Humpers: A low grade of roadies chosen for their ability to carry enormous gear up long flights of spiral stairs.

It's engaged: It's busy.

Keen: Enthusiastic, as in teacher's pet.

Knackered: Really really tired out.

Knickers: Panties, but much bigger and made of much thicker stuff, like maybe canvas.

Lairy: Given to nicking stuff. *See also* pinch *and* nick.

Laminates: Backstage passes, eagerly sought after by all fans.

Lav: Short for "lavatory," as in washroom, restroom, powder room, and all that.

Lift: Elevator.

Lord Harry (by the): A long-forgotten English aristocrat now used only in exclamations of amazement.

Lorra lorra: A huge amount of something, particularly used in the world of rock management, as in "a lot of lot of."

Lorries: Trucks.

Manky: Worn, tired, ragged. Possibly from the French *manque,* but possibly not.

Mooch: Somewhere between a slouch and a slump.

Naff off: Not very polite way of saying "Get lost."

Nattering: Chattering.

Nick: Pinch, half-inch, swipe. All right, *steal.*

Niffy: A niff is an odor given off by anoraks (see above) or other non-fragrant items.

Night bear: I have no idea what one of these is, but there is one tattooed on Eric's back, and it is absolutely terrifying.

Nip round: Go swiftly around.

Nippers: Children (or ankle biters).

Noughts: Zeroes.

Pegging it: Like legging it, but a bit faster.

Petrol: Gas.

Pinch: Steal. (In Cockney rhyming slang, half-inch = pinch.) *See also* nick.

Plumber's mate: Don't you have plumbers in America, to fix your pipe? And do they not have mates, or helpers, who hold the wrench while the plumber drinks the coffee? Thought so.

Punters: Clients, as in festival-goers.

Quad bike: Somewhat like an all-terrain motorbike with four wheels.

Quid: Pound. See *also* squids.

Quiz machine: Machine found in rural places that asks general knowledge questions and gives out money for right answers.

Ribena: Blood-colored black currant syrup, much loved by British children and a great disappointment to many vampires.

Ring: Call on the phone.

Saveloy: Luckily for Americans, there is no such food concept as a Saveloy in the U.S. Think of a thick-skinned, extra fat wiener crammed with essence of dead dog.

Scoffed: Eating in a violent manner.

Shopping trolley: Shopping cart.

Shurrup: Shut up.

Singlet: Tank top undershirt.

Skint: Broke. (In Cockney rhyming slang, Boracic Lint = skint.)

Skittle alley: Long, narrow room where a primitive form of ten-pin bowling takes place, using nine pins.

Squids: Marine animals. Also, a way of saying "quids." One quid is one pound sterling, which is money, of course.

Spotty: A spot is a zit.

Storm-wrack: A very poetic way of saying the kind of clouds that mean really bad weather, like tornadoes.

Tackety boots: Workboots with steel cleats in the soles. Listen to them in your mind. *Tacketa, tacketa,* right?

They've lost their bottle: "Bottle" is another word for "nerve," innit.

Trainers: Sneakers.

Tranny: Short for Transit, which is short for Ford Transit, which is the truck that has carried British rock and roll out of the dark ages and into the present day.

Verges: Grass strips on the edge of the highway.

Waggish: Awfully amusing.

WI Tea Things Rota: The list or schedule used by the WI or Women's Institute, a club of tough British women, for doing the dishes after their teas . . . aah, forgeddit.

Windscreen: Windshield.

Wonga: Mazuma, sovs, folding green. Money, in other words.

THE RETURN OF DEATH ERIC
APOCALYPSE? WOW!
TOUR CONTEST

You could win an
iTUNES GIFT CARD
and rock your own
headbanging soundtrack!

HOW? TELL US WHAT BAND SHOULD OPEN FOR DEATH ERIC—AND WHY.

Ten Grand Prize winners will receive
an **iTunes™ Music Card** worth $25.

Send your entry via e-mail to:
children.publicity@bloomsburyusa.com,
subject line: Death Eric Contest
or by U.S. mail to:
Death Eric Contest
c/o Walker Books for Young Readers
Marketing Department
104 Fifth Avenue, 7th Floor
New York, NY 10011

ROCK ON AND WIN!

(Turn the page for official rules)

The Official Rules:

HOW TO ENTER

NO PURCHASE NECESSARY. Contest begins November 1, 2006, and ends April 1, 2007. Enter by printing your name, date of birth, parent's/guardian's name if you're under the age of 18, full address, and phone number on an 8-1/2 x 11" sheet of paper or via e-mail and describe in 200 words or fewer what band should open for Death Eric on their Apocalypse? WOW! Tour and your reasons for choosing them. Mail to: Death Eric Contest, c/o Walker Books for Young Readers, Marketing Department, 104 Fifth Avenue, 7th Floor, New York, NY 10011 or e-mail to children.publicity@bloomsburyusa.com, subject line: Death Eric Contest. Entries must be received by Walker no later than April 1, 2007. Partially completed or illegible entries will not be accepted. Sponsor will not be responsible for lost, late, mutilated, illegible, stolen, incomplete or misdirected entries, or entries with postage due. All entries become the property of Walker and will not be returned, so please keep a copy for your records.

ELIGIBILITY

Contest is open to legal residents of the United States and Canada, excluding Quebec, Puerto Rico, Guam, the U.S. Virgin Islands, and where prohibited by law, to persons over eight (8) years of age. All federal, state, and local laws and regulations apply. Void wherever prohibited or restricted by law. Employees (and employees' immediate family and household members) of Sponsor, and its parent, affiliates, subsidiaries, suppliers, printers, distributors, advertising and promotional agencies, and prize suppliers are not eligible to participate in the Contest.

PRIZES

There will be ten (10) Grand Prize winners selected. Grand Prize winners will win an iTunes™ Music Card. Approximate retail value of each Grand Prize: $25.00 U.S; total approximate value of prizes: $250.00. No prize substitution except by Sponsor due to unavailability.

WINNERS

All eligible entries received by the end of the contest closing date will be selected by the Walker Marketing Department. All entries submitted in accordance with the submission guidelines contained in these Official Rules will be judged on the basis of creativity, clarity of presentation, and uniqueness of style. Winners will be notified by phone or e-mail on or about May 15, 2007. Any winner notification not responded to or returned as undeliverable may result in prize forfeiture and an alternate winner shall be selected. The potential prize winner and, if the potential prize winner is under the age of 18, the potential prize winner's parent or guardian will be required to sign and return an affidavit of eligibility and release of liability within fourteen (14) days of notification. In the event of noncompliance within this time period or if the prize is returned, refused, or returned as undeliverable, then an additional judging from eligible entries will be made to determine an alternate winner. No substitution or transfer of a prize is permitted except by Walker.

RESERVATIONS

By participating, Winner (and if under the age of 18, the Winner's parent/legal guardian) agrees that Bloomsbury/Walker and its parent companies assigns, subsidiaries or affiliates, advertising, promotion, fulfillment agencies, and suppliers will have no liability whatsoever, and will be held harmless by Winner (and Winner's parent/legal guardian) for any liability for any injuries, losses, or damages of any kind to person, including death, and property resulting in whole or in part, directly or indirectly, from the acceptance, possession, misuse, or use of the prize, or participation in the contest. By entering the contest, Winner (and if under the age of 18, Winner's parent or legal guardian) consents to the use of Winner's name, likeness, and biographical data for publicity and promotional purposes on behalf of Bloomsbury/Walker with no additional compensation or further permission (except where prohibited by law). For the names of the winners, available after May 15, 2007, please send a stamped, self-addressed envelope to: Walker Books for Young Readers, Death Eric Contest Winners, 104 Fifth Avenue, 7th Floor, New York, NY 10011.